D1452875

AFSANEH

Also by Kaveh Basmenji published by Saqi

Tehran Blues: Youth Culture in Iran

AFSANEH

SHORT STORIES BY IRANIAN WOMEN

Edited and translated by
Kaveh Basmenji

SAQI

British Library Cataloguing-in-Publication Date
A catalogue record of this book is available from the British Library

ISBN 0-86356-572-7
EAN 9-780863-565724

This edition first published 2005

Saqi Books
26 Westbourne Grove
London W2 5RH
www.saqibooks.com

Contents

A Legacy of Survival

In the strict sense of the term, 'stories by women writers' began to appear only in the first half of the twentieth century, when Iranian society experienced radical changes in the wake of the Constitutional Movement, which sought to put an end to centuries of absolute rule. Inspired by political developments in the Western world, the intellectual leaders of the Movement aimed at modernising Iran in all respects. According to Ann K.S. Lambton, the Constitutional Revolution marked the end of the medieval period in Iran, although its objectives were marred by the chaos and civil war that it entailed.[1] As part of the widespread drive for modernisation, educated women from aristocratic backgrounds began to plant the seeds of struggle for women's rights in a country whose traditions had previously confined women to the household and required them to be obedient servants.

Prior to 1931, there is only one mention of a female writer within Persian literature: the mythical story-teller Sheherezad of *The Book*

---

1.   Ann K.S. Lambton, *Qajar Persia: Eleven Studies*, I.B.Tauris, 1987, p. ix.

of One Thousand and One Nights. Also known as *The Book of a Thousand Nights and a Night, 1001 Arabian Nights,* or simply the *Arabian Nights,* the book has become a piece of classic Arabic literature. Many of the stories, however, are thought to have originally been collected from folk tales of Persia and later compiled to include stories from various other authors. Legend has it that Shahriar (meaning 'king' in Persian), king of an unnamed island 'between India and China', is so shocked by his wife's infidelity that he kills her and, believing all women to be likewise unfaithful, orders his *vizier* (meaning 'minister' in Persian) to provide him with a new wife every night (in some versions, every third night). After spending one night with his bride, the king has her executed at dawn. This practice continues unabated, until the *vizier's* clever daughter Sheherezad (meaning 'City-born' in Persian) forms a plan and volunteers to become Shahriar's next wife. Every night after their wedding, she spends hours telling him stories, each ending at dawn with a cliff-hanger, so the king will commute the execution out of a desire to hear the rest of the tale. Her plan is so successful that she gives birth to three sons, and the king is convinced of her faithfulness.

The tales vary widely: they include historical tales, love stories, tragedies, comedies, poems, burlesques and Muslim religious legends. Some of the famous stories Scheherazad spins appear in many western translations as *Alladin's Lamp, Sindbad the Sailor,* and the tale of *Ali Baba and the Forty Thieves.*

In a symbolic continuation of Sheherezad's tradition, modern Iranian women tell stories as a means of survival, albeit intellectual, rather than physical survival. In their quest to attain new forms of expression and ways of describing the world they live in, Iranian women writers suffer from a double burden. While Persian literature in general has been constrained by traditional dogmas and taboos as well as by socio-political circumstances, Iranian women have also been restricted in their experience of the public sphere. In other words, they have less potential than male writers to cultivate their writing as a profession.

According to Elaine Showalter's theory of Gynocriticism, there have been three phases of female literary evolution in the West: the Feminine phase, the Feminist phase, and the Female phase. During the Feminine phase (1840–80), women wrote in an attempt to equal the intellectual achievements of the male writers. One sign of this stage was the popularity among women authors of the male pseudonym. Female English writers such as George Eliot used masculine camouflage beyond the name itself. The tone, structure, and other elements of their writing were also affected by their struggle to overcome the literary double standard. American writers, too, used pseudonyms. These women, however, chose superfeminine names, such as Fanny Fern, in order to disguise their 'boundless energy, powerful economic motives, and keen professional skills'.[1]

During the second stage of literary evolution, the Feminist phase (1880–1920), women rejected 'the accommodating postures of femininity' and used literature 'to dramatize the ordeals of wronged womanhood'. Writing from this period often dramatizes the social injustice suffered by women. Other texts fantasize about the utopian possibilities of female societies, e.g. Amazonian or suffragette communities.[2]

This 'Feminist Socialist Realism' has given way to the Female phase, in progress since 1920. Writers of the Female phase reject what those of the Feminine and Feminist stages promote because these both depended on masculinity and were ironically male-oriented. Literature of the Female phase turns instead to female experience as the source of an autonomous art, extending the feminist analysis of culture to the forms and techniques of literature.[3]

The evolution of women's prose literature in Iran has followed roughly the same pattern as the one outlined by Elaine Showalter in *A Literature of Their Own* which I describe above. With the advent

---

1. Elaine Showalter, *A Literature of Their Own*, Princeton University Press, Princeton, 1977; pp. 27–28.
2. *A Literature of Their Own*, p. 29.
3. *A Literature of Their Own*, p. 33.

of a modern state in Iran under the rule of Reza Shah Pahlavi in the 1920s, women began to play a more active role in society. Although few major changes occurred in the legal position of women during the rule of Reza Shah (1924–41), the new regime put considerable emphasis on education, including that of women, as a major vehicle for modernisation. This boosted the number of schools for girls and also provided opportunities for educated women to be employed as teachers.

Thus prose writing by women authors dates back to the beginning of the modern epoch in Iran, circa 1930s, when along with a hoard of other breakthroughs, including secularization of the civil code, girls were allowed to attend schools and be admitted to universities.

During the two following decades (1940s–50s), fifteen women writers entered the literary arena with novels and short stories, against 270 male writers of fiction[1]. These included sensationalist renditions of social conditions as well as historical pulp fiction. During this period, women were chiefly involved in a struggle for basic rights in society, and therefore literature was not a top priority for them. As a result, hardly a work of any considerable literary value was published, and most of the novels and short stories followed the examples set by male writers. Nevertheless, pioneering women, mostly from aristocratic families, were busy starting modern girls' schools and women's foundations, as well as periodicals dedicated to women's issues. This had a tremendous impact on women's literature of later generations.

The 1960s, one of the most flourishing times for modern culture in general and prose literature in particular, witnessed the emergence of some twenty-five women writers of fiction, as against 130 male authors, showing a considerable increase in the ratio of female/ male authors. In pace with general trends in society, including the growth in education and job opportunities, as well as the gain of greater rights in the domestic sphere, more and more women turned to arts and literature. In this period, works by women writers began

---

1.   Hassan Mirabedini, *Baran Quarterly*, vols 4–5, October 2004.

to show signs of a mature artistic creativity. They examined the
state of the 'second sex' rather than merely duplicating romantic
clichés like the women writers of previous decades. Nevertheless,
the major subject of the stories published in this period remained
the sufferings of women in a patriarchal, male-dominated society,
mostly depicted in a naturalist style. This approach is meaningfully
formulated in the words of Mrs Principal in 'To Whom Shall I Say
Hello?': 'Women intrinsically belong to the working class.'The most
prominent writers of this period include Simin Daneshvar, Mahshid
Amirshahy, Goli Taraqqi, Mihan Bahrami and Mehri Yalfani.

Simin Daneshvar, born in 1931, arguably remains the most
famous of all Iranian women authors ever published. One recurring
theme in most of her stories is the oppressive atmosphere prevailing
in Iran during the last two decades before the Revolution of 1979.
'To Whom Shall I Say Hello?' is a brilliant example of a narrative
exploring the plight of women in a male-dominated society. It is
an account of a lonely old woman's reflections of her past, her
daughter's hard life and her own solitude.

Mahshid Amirshahy, also born in 1931, was one of the pioneering
Iranian women writers both in the selection of her subject matter
and its treatment. Whether describing childhood memories in rich,
albeit shattered families, exploring the psyche of Iranian women and
their emotional world or giving accounts of doomed relationships,
her writing is characterised by her ability to create atmosphere and
a transparent, immediate narrative style.

Goli Taraqqi, born in 1941, mostly writes about characters who
are sick, hopeless and desperate people leading lonely lives, fearing
everything. 'The Shemiran Bus' and 'A House in Heaven' are among
her best works, and probably two of the most shining examples of
Iran's contemporary prose literature. In the words of one critic,
'If Taraqqi had not written anything but these stories, she would
still be regarded as one of the first-rate Iranian writers.'[1] In 'The

---

1.   Susan Gaviri, *Dar Astaneh-ye Fasli Sard* [On The Threshold of a Cold
      Season], Rowshangaran Publishers, Tehran, 1998, p. 11.

Shemiran Bus', first published in the 1960s, she describes a simple but deep friendship between a little girl and a macho bus driver. In 'A House in Heaven', she tells the story of a family whose lives have been shattered by the Iran-Iraq war and immigration.

Between 1970 and 1990, the ratio of the female/male writers remained constant at about one to five. However, as the Islamic Revolution of 1979 shook the political, economic and social foundations of Iran to their feet, it introduced a drastic and dramatic change into contemporary prose literature. One of the most notable writers in the years leading up to the Revolution was Shahrnoosh Parsipour. Born in 1946 she became one of the pioneers of magic realism and one of the most controversial female Iranian writers. She often describes the anguish rooted in the historical and traditional legacy of women as the inferior sex from the viewpoint of a disturbed, distorted mind. The main characters in her stories are pathetic girls and women who, in order to escape their boring and absurd lives, seek refuge in nature or in the grave. Almost all the characters of the collection titled *Crystal Pendants* (1977) are lonely people alienated by life and immersed in their fantasies. In most of Parsipour's stories, there is no distinction between life and death; the house and the cemetery are interconnected, and it is hard to tell reality from fantasy. However, her world is not always bleak; she is also a skilful creator of poetic atmospheres, an outstanding example being 'Mahdokht'. The late Ghazaleh Alizadeh (1946–96) also dealt in her stories and novels with female characters mired by incurable obsessions and anxieties, existing in a world of self-deception and desperation.

The Islamic Revolution and the 1980–88 Iran-Iraq war were reflected obliquely in the works of post-1979 writers, as state censorship underwent a change in content and criteria. Under the Shah, revolt against traditional dogma was not as harshly treated as any allusion to political dissent. Notwithstanding the predominantly masculine culture, as a result of the drive for modernisation, women writers were able to describe their resentment of, and disillusionment with, society and draw picture of private fantasies. It was more often than not, within such a framework, that political criticism was expressed, if indirectly. With the advent of a religious state after the Revolution, however, a new hoard of taboos was added to the list. Although the new restrictions applied to male and female writers alike, it was women writers who were most constrained, as any mention of, for instance, carnal desire would be considered much more 'indecent' and 'shameful' if expressed by a female author, and therefore dealt with more strictly.

Nevertheless, as the Revolution brought women to the forefront of society, a new generation of female writers began to test the boundaries of censorship in their quest to express themselves through art and literature. A number of authors chose to throw a light on the large-scale problems of being a woman in a patriarchal, moralist, religious society by describing personal or family situations as cross-sections of a larger picture. Meanwhile, others opted for stream-of-consciousness or magic realism as a means of portraying the dilemmas and woes of women's lives. In 'The Little Secret', for example, Farkhondeh Aqaei gives a powerful account of the horrors – and at the same time, the boredom of living in 1980s Iran through the everyday events of a hospital ward. Conversely, Moniru Ravanipour describes the plight of women in the surrealistic atmosphere of poor fishing villages of southern Iran in *Kanizu, Heart of Steel*, and *Siria, Siria*.

In the 1990s the number of women writers showed a thirteen-fold increase as compared to the two previous decades, indicating a ratio of one to 1.5 against their male counterparts.[1] The period, epitomised by the end of the War with Iraq and the relative relaxation of social restrictions, was also marked by the emergence of a new generation of women writing romantic, escapist and entertaining stories: something that had hitherto been practically impossible. Many became nationwide bestsellers with unprecedented circulations, mostly appearing in the form of the novel. The sphere

1 Hassan Mirabedini, *Baran Quarterly*, vols 4–5, October 2004.

of the short story to a large extent remained the domain of writers of serious literature. This period is chiefly characterised by a neo-realistic approach to the subject matter, exploring the situation of characters that are mostly victims of society.

The stories in this collection have been picked from both pre- and post-Revolutionary periods. However, for the most part, the stories are united by their portrayal of women characters blighted by solitude and desperation of one kind or another, leading estranged lives in a male-dominated society. Some of them take refuge in their memories, particularly in childhood memories; others struggle in hopeless situations: old women neglected by their own children and sent to old people's houses; housewives at the mercy of violent, egotistical, or at best insensitive men; young girls suffering from emotional emptiness caused by incomprehensible traditions.

It is not mere coincidence that the 'evil' male characters outnumber the 'good' ones by a large proportion. Interestingly, out of roughly twenty-three main male characters in the stories here, only seven are painted in a clearly positive light – and of these seven, three are dead, and four have only an ethereal, ghost-like or imaginary existence, either in memory or in fantasy. In contrast, most of the male characters in the stories exhibit traits of wickedness, ignorance, indifference, insensitiveness or helplessness in their treatment of women. Clear examples are ruthless, violent husbands and fathers in 'To Whom Shall I Say Hello?', 'Midnight Drum', 'The Stranger', and 'The Grandmother'. In many cases the implications are that the "wicked" male is himself a victim of tradition and conditioning, or subject to a blind fate. The disinherited peasant in 'O, Baba! O, Baba!' and the disabled soldier in 'The Little Secret' are among the few living male characters that enjoy the full sympathy of the writers.

This cynical perception of men is predominant even when writers are describing modern, educated couples. In 'A House in Heaven', 'although a calm and reasonable man, Massoud D. suddenly blew a gasket for no obvious reason; he shouted and everyone heard his shouts; the kids panicked'. In 'Midnight Drum', the narrator is obviously disgusted with performing the sexual act with her husband: 'Tonight, the night of relief from submission, she should be at peace. The nights he's at home, the nights she keeps wandering in the kitchen until he goes to sleep, the nights she pretends to be sick or weary, the nights she submits without passion or love, or the nights she surrenders to the raw and unrefined need of her own body – the nights smeared with deceit and hypocrisy or fear and submission – on such nights it's no wonder there's no trace of peace.' Similarly, in 'Like a Well', the narrator's husband is inquisitive, insensitive and only interested in sex.

Another common feature of the stories of this collection – and women's stories in general – is that little, if any, direct reference is made to earthly love and carnal relations. Again, this can be attributed to the conditions of the society in which the writers have been living and the unwritten codes they have been constrained by – both before and after the Islamic Revolution of 1979. The only exception here is the short contact between two strangers in 'Khorramshahr-Tehran', which also represents one of the rare instances where female and male characters are, so to speak, equally defying those codes.

In a 1999 interview published in the French daily *Libération*, Monique Wittig said, 'For me, there is no such thing as "women's literature"; it doesn't exist. One is either a writer, or one isn't. In the writer's imagination, gender is irrelevant. It is a place where one finds complete freedom. Language makes this possible. The idea is to construct a sexually neutral zone; to escape the confines of gender.' Nevertheless, the bulk of the works of literature produced by contemporary Iranian women writers tends to draw a division along gender lines, although in many cases a very subtle one. Therefore, despite wide differences in literary approaches and prose styles, the common feature among the stories in the present volume is a precise and sincere depiction of the lives, emotions and attitudes of female characters.

Kaveh Basmenji

SIMIN DANESHVAR

To Whom Shall I Say Hello?

Who is indeed left that I can say hello to? Mrs Principal is dead, Haj Esmail is missing, my only daughter has fallen into the claws of a wolf ... The cat died, coal tongs fell on the spider, and the spider died too ... And now, what a snow is falling! Whenever it snows I get so depressed that I'd like to bang my head against the wall. The health insurance doctor said, 'Whenever you're depressed, get out.' He said, 'Whenever you feel sad and there's noone you can share your sadness with, talk to yourself loudly.' Meaning that you have to become your own agony aunt. He said, 'Go to the desert and shout, swear at anybody you want to ...' Oh, what a snow, first it was swirling and scattering, now it's falling in tiny flakes and the way it's falling it's obvious it will not abate so soon; it's been snowing like this since early winter ...

And the leftover snow was frozen on the ground, and where could people dump the snow that was on their roofs if not into back alleys? Coming and going was what the strong sportsmen, young athletes and mindless kids whose schools had been closed would do. If it didn't snow, there would be inflation and there would be famine and they would speak of rationing water and electricity; and if it did snow, life and schools would be closed.

Last night there was a blackout at Ala'ei Street, and Kowkab Soltan, who was sitting under the *korsi*[1] and gazing at the darkness, freaked out. Her heart pounded with anxiety, as if someone was washing clothes in her stomach. She thought she would go insane if she didn't get out of the room and out of the darkness. She got up, fumbled her way across the room and made her way out of the cold dark house, to stand outside the door. A cold wind was blowing and the neighbour's child was crying. Two nights before, their water pipe had burst; it had been three days since the garbage man had collected the garbage.

Kowkab Soltan, a retired employee of the ministry of education, didn't have much garbage to be taken away. The bursting of the water pipe had not inflicted much damage on her belongings either. Her room was on the second floor, next to Mr Panirpour's room; he had at his disposal two large rooms, a kitchen and a lavatory; he had three ripe daughters and a giant of a wife. It was the neighbours that had nicknamed him Panirpour[2] (because he sold dairy products at Jaleh Street, and he did not sell to anyone on credit, not even you) though his real name was Mr Shahriatpour-Yazdani. For ablutions and defecation, Kowkab Soltan would go downstairs and take water from the tap in the kitchen; she didn't have much cooking to do either: her tooth constantly irritated her gums and tongue. Her room was the size of a hand's palm, with no furniture; she had sent all her belongings to her son-in-law's house as dowry.

Kowkab Soltan came out from under the *korsi* and stood at the window to watch the snow. The rooftops had already turned completely white, and snow had settled on the pine tree in the neighbour's garden also. The icicles hanging from the opposite

---

1. A low wooden stool covered with a large quilt, under which a brazier of burning charcoal is put to warm the bodies of those sitting round the stool.

2. Literally, *panir* means 'cheese', and *pour* means 'son'.

roof had been there yesterday, and the day before; they had been there since the beginning of Sagittarius.[1] How heavy was her heart; the thought of Haj Esmail had not left her head since last night.

'What fun we had together; alas, it passed so quickly. He taught me how to read and write. I used to read *Amir Arsalan* for him. We read *Amir Arsalan* five times, *Shams-e Qahqaheh* three times, *Azra's Kiss* twice. Mrs Principal had loads of books; we would take her books and return them later. Haj Esmail was the school's janitor, and I served Mrs Principal from my own home. Poor woman had few demands: I peeled pomegranates and took them to the school at ten o'clock, and when pomegranates weren't around, I took sherbet for her; I cooked lunch but in the evenings she didn't have dinner, she just drank a glass of milk and went to bed. Good God, we had every pleasure that there was to be had in this town, we went so many times to theatre halls and cinemas! We saw *The Thief of Baghdad, Hansa the Arab, Secrets of New York, Arshin Malalan* – four or five times each! Our money was blessed; Mrs Principal paid my wages, Haj Esmail got his salary from the ministry.

It was the health insurance doctor himself who said: talk to yourself, pour out whatever makes you happy or has made you sad. Don't keep these things in your heart …

We went to Karbala, we begged of Imam Hossein to have kids. God gave us Robabeh. It was the year after that Haj Esmail went to work one morning but didn't come back in the evening. As simple as that, the big fellow went missing. Mrs Principal, the security, police, all searched for Haj Esmail. I myself hugged Robabeh and went from one office to another, but it was as if there never had been a Haj Esmail; he disappeared. I would put Robabeh to sleep and sit on my own, smoking opium. I had made Mrs Principal's cat addicted to opium; as soon as the smell of opium rose, she came and sat by me, closed her eyes and snored. I blew smoke at her; she twisted and turned. The cat died of natural causes. Then I made a spider addicted. It had woven a web in the corner of the room. As

---

1.   Corresponding to 23 November –22 December.

the smell of opium rose, it would come down and not move from near the brazier. The coal tongs fell on it. It died too.

Mrs Principal wrote an application letter, made me the janitor in her school in place of Haj Esmail and kept me in her house until she died. God bless her soul. She said, 'Your work has doubled, but so much the better! You can make this long, friendless life bearable only by hard work.' She was cross at my opium smoking, though. She nagged so much that I lost interest in opium. Besides, I had so much work to do that there was no time to smoke opium. In Mrs Principal's house I did her domestic work and at the school I cleaned the lavatories, took the girls' reports to their houses and got tips; near New Year's Eve I planted labdanum in ceramic pots; I grew wheat sprouts in clay vases, I grew lentil sprouts and took them into Mrs Principal's room or to the teachers' houses ... I got tips from ten to twenty toomans. I did all these things so that Robabeh could live in peace and comfort. I dressed her like girls from noble families, until she got her diploma. I wouldn't have made her get married had Mrs Principal not died. But Mrs Principal died and I became a vagrant. They made me retire after eighteen years of work. They said, 'Your time has come,' and threw me out of Mrs Principal's house. I was forced to ruin the girl's life, to give her to this mean bastard who works in Mr Lachini's notary and doesn't give a damn about anybody. What can I do? The girl was pretty and dressed up like girls from noble families; she also went to the hairdresser's every week. With retirement pension and in a rented room, it wasn't possible to carry on like that anymore. And she didn't pass the university entry exam.

The health insurance doctor said, 'Swear loudly at anybody you want to, so that your head cools off.' And now my mouth's always full of curses. God only knows that I used to be a romantic; I used to like streams and trees and meadows and the moon in the sky. Nobody's taught me praying and fasting and murmuring spells; when we were in Karbala, I said my prayers while I stood behind Haj Esmail; he said them loud and I said them in my heart. I forgot them when we came back to Tehran. Instead, I know how to swear. I swear at all the 'unmen' and the mean people of the world; to all those men who later became unmen and the nice ones who became nasty; I curse them. Many remained good, stood by their word and died; many disappeared. God bless everyone's deceased ones. Mrs Principal said: our misery is that we turn men into unmen. She said: they suck our blood through pipe-like veins, making us bloodless and unmen.

They brought Aqa Reza into the gathering; noblemen, aristocrats and heavyweights were sitting all around. They kept saying, 'Aqa Reza, say, "Hello!"' He asked, 'To whom shall I say hello?'

I might as well get up and go buy some milk to make rice pudding. No, I'll make plain pudding. But how shall I go out in this freezing weather? The new American Bella boots I have just bought are too big for my feet. My tooth irritates my mouth, my right knee is in pain; the thought of Haj Esmail hasn't left me for a moment since last night, noises rattle in my head. But I must get out, I'll go insane if I sit on my own in this room and talk to myself. Someone is clawing at my entrails again. I'll wrap newspapers around my ankles, on top of them I'll put on those woollen socks I have woven myself, and then the boots will fit my feet. How helpful knitting is in these times; how nicely it distracts you from thoughts and fancies. I've so far knitted ten woollen children's jumpers for Mansour and Massoud. What beautiful designs I've put in them! But he's forbidden them to accept gifts from me. Now I just keep knitting and ripping it all up. I don't have anyone to knit for, nor have I any spare money to spend; all the prices have gone up, skyrocketed; it's only human life that's cheap.

That very first day I said that the only thing I had in this world was this one child. It's against God's mercy to take my child away from me; but that jackass wanted a fight from the beginning; otherwise why did he rent a house in Bagh-e Saba to be far away from me? And then when I uttered a couple of words in all honesty, he grabbed my hand and threw me out of my daughter's house. I know what to do: I'll go learn the Scandal Prayers from Mrs Panirpour; I'll put my pants on top of my head, go to the roof of the lavatory and do the Scandal Prayers against my wretched son-in-law. I'll curse him! Mrs Panirpour knows all sorts of prayers. Didn't she – the other day on the rooftop – tell me to do the Scandal Prayers? On Thursday evenings they listen to Mr Rashed's sermons; they turn up the volume of their radio so that the neighbours can also hear it. I like to hear Qamarolmoluk Vaziri sing, she sings like a nightingale. Mrs Principal had a few Qamarolmoluk Vaziri records; I don't know who inherited them. In summertime, God bless her soul, she would go to Evin-Darakeh; the school was closed too. We sprinkled water in the courtyard, watered the garden petunias we had planted ourselves, sat under the vine trellis, wound the gramophone, put on a Qamarolmoluk record, a Zelli record or Eqbalossoltan. I made lemon sherbet and gave it to Haj Esmail and told him: 'Enjoy it, dear!' She said: 'You drink first ...' What a load would be taken off my heart if only Robabeh came to pay me a brief visit and brought Mansour and Massoud with her. I told Massoud: 'Massoud, you cutie pie!' He said: 'Cutie pie yourself!' I begged him to give a kiss to his grandma; he turned his face to my lips. Scandal Prayers should be said on the rooftop of lavatory, the sun should be up; afterwards Moaviyyeh and Yazid should be cursed. Mrs Panirpour said this. Before winter, she had come to the rooftop and sat there cleaning green herbs; the sunshine was pleasant; I had also gone up there, to hang out the washing. My heart was so heavy that I went to her to say hello. That day we chattered and unburdened ourselves; I told her that I had had all the fun in the world and played all the tricks. Then I told her of my son-in-law and how he had made a hell out of my life. She said: 'Say Scandal Prayers so that God will scandalise him.' I don't know why she became cross with me from that day on; if we happened to run into each other, she pretended to have not seen me in all her life; so I didn't say hello to her any more. Despite that I'll go to her and learn Scandal Prayers from her. I wish it were sunny and there weren't so much snow on the lavatory's rooftop. God has shaken His torn quilt; the cotton from His huge quilt has fallen everywhere, and is still falling. May God forgive me! Oh no, I've become soft in the head; I'll never be human again. All these miseries come to you because you have uttered so much blasphemy!

All I said was: 'For Devil's sake, you call yourself a man? You and those jackass brothers of yours have killed my poor kid. The nine-month pregnant woman has in one hand the child's lunchbox, that bastard Massoud's hand in the other; she washes the clothes of all of you, she irons, cooks lunch, cooks dinner. Your mother only plays with her rosary beads and issues orders; your brothers act as if she is their slave. You yourself, coming back from the notary, which I pray to God you never did, are like a carcass; my poor child brings warm water and washes your feet, rubs your corns with pumice stone. I have seen it myself with these very eyes that I wish had gone blind ...'

Whenever we went to visit them I went there like a queen and came back like a tramp. He would browbeat me so much, her mother humiliated me and my child so much, and his brothers giggled and laughed so much that I got fed up with life. I went there seldom. One day I went to Massoud's kindergarten to see my child. I saw Robabeh holding in one hand the kid's lunchbox and a shopping bag, and holding Massoud's hand in the other; a nine-month pregnant woman; slipping on the snow and walking, and Massoud nagging, 'Mommy, lift me up, lift me up!' I lifted the kid up instead and we went to their damn house together. The thug was lying there under the *korsi*, munching roasted seeds. His mother was saying her goddamn prayers in a corner of the room. His brothers had not come yet. I said: 'You call yourself a man? Can't you darn well go fetch your kid from the kindergarten?' I unzipped my mouth and told him whatever damn thing I could. He was petrified with shock; he came out from under the *korsi* and yanked my hand and dragged me out of the room and threw me out of the door. He called me wretched demon, termagant hag, shrew witch! What names he called me ...

And besides, he's a brute; he beats up my daughter. I've heard it from neighbours. I've heard that he's said: 'Isn't it true that your mom has brought you up by working as a servant and a janitor?' I've even heard that my daughter has given birth to Mansour without the help of a midwife. He must be twenty-months old by now; he must be speaking by now. I've heard that his mother said, 'What does the second birth need a midwife for?' And that she delivered the child herself. I could no longer take it when I heard all that. I got up, bought three kilos of tangerines and went to visit my daughter. Her face was as yellow as turmeric; what a colour, what a condition; she could not even force herself to sit up in bed. She begged me not to stay there, 'Mom, get up and go, and take the tangerines with you. He'll beat me up if he gets wind of the fact that you've been here, and I won't be able to get out of bed for God knows how long.' Tons of dirty clothes were heaped up. I went berserk. I said, 'Robabeh, may your mother die for you, this is not what life's supposed to be; this is death. Your father – God bless his soul – and I had all the fun in the world; why should you suffer and keep your mouth shut? How many lives will we be given? Your dad wrapped you up, sang you lullabies, washed you and took you out.' She said, 'Mom, I've got two kids, I can't get divorced; besides, he doesn't treat me bad.' I said, 'You needn't have studied so much if you wanted to become a servant ...'

Oh, Robabeh, whom do you think you're fooling? What other misery did you expect him to bring to you? He's also forbidden me to go to Massoud's school. I go to the butcher's, the grocer's and the dairy shop near their house so that I can see one of my child's neighbours. They must see her or hear the voice of that ribald bitch. I've heard that Robabeh's become bespectacled because she studied so much. Oh, what do you know, maybe he's hit my child on the head and that's why she's become bespectacled! Oh, the things I hear. I've heard that he's broken my child's head, that he's beaten Massoud, that the kid's ear has bled; I've heard ... I utter such curses against him that if only one of them worked, he would be done forever; but that's the way it is: the bully always remains healthy.

Oh, Robabeh, your father and I had all the fun in the world, and I didn't deny you anything. I wanted you to be spared hard work as long as you lived in my house, knowing that you'd have to work hard when you got married, but I couldn't have known so much. His mean, cheeky sisters go to camp in Mamma's house whenever they fall sick. To hell with Mamma; to the devil with Mamma! And who takes care of them? Robabeh of course. 'Robabeh! Hurry up and bring fruit juice; hurry up and cook chicken stew; hurry up and buy some milk; warm it and give it to us to shove it up ours!' Mrs Principal – God bless her soul – would say: 'You're raising this kid in eiderdown; you let her have time for her lessons; you try to lift her up out of her class; but what you don't know is that women intrinsically belong to the working class.' God bless your soul, woman; how wise you were!

I might as well get up and go buy some milk to make rice pudding. No, I'll make plain pudding. This goddamn tooth is awfully painful. The health insurance doctor said: 'Get out of the house whenever loneliness is making you freak out ...'

She stood up and looked into the mirror. The roots of her hair had whitened, further up the hairs turned reddish and the tips were pitch black. Her son-in-law had not called her a shrew witch without reason. But he didn't know that when you sigh, white hairs protrude from your heart. When she had Robabeh in her womb, the top of her heart itched during the ninth month of pregnancy. Mrs Principal said, 'The child is growing hair.' She said, 'The child's hair sprouts from her mother's heart.' She said, 'Any way you look at it, women intrinsically belong to the working class.'

She lifted up the corner of the quilt. She took one tooman from under the pileless rug. What a pity she had included those two Kurdish carpets and sent them to the house of such a son-in-law. She put on her praying *chador* and came out of the courtyard door holding her *jujube* red umbrella. She walked cautiously, groping at the wall, the tin drainpipe and the windows of people's houses. She wished she had had her tooth extracted, but she didn't want to appear before people toothless and with all those wrinkles. She had to walk down the whole Ala'ei Street, then turn round by the Planning Organisation; there were all sorts of shops in Shah Abad Street. She could walk by the police station to Jaleh Street and buy some milk from Mr Panirpour's dairy shop.

There was no milk left; neither bottled milk, nor carton milk, nor ordinary milk. 'Oh, Tehran, may you be destroyed, may you collapse on the heads of the mean and the unmen and the castrated ones; with these hard cold winters and hot dry summers of yours. Neither a river, nor any trees, nor a stream. As Mrs Principal said: spread like an ink stain on blotting paper; running in every direction, clawing at the surroundings like a crab. May you be destroyed, you crazy crab town!'

She went to the butchers. Mr Panirpour's wife was buying meat. She had ordered a leg of mutton. Aqa Jafar was chopping the leg and breaking the bones in two with a cleaver. It was nicely coloured non-frozen Iranian lamb meat. She said: 2 kilos and 700 grams. 'Well, people don't get roly-poly and grow double chins without good reason.' Mrs Panirpour was wearing a woollen headscarf, she was wearing gloves, on top of her jacket and skirt she was wearing a sheepskin coat. She took a fifty-tooman bill out of her coat pocket and handed it to Aqa Jafar. He had cut his hand, and the piece of cloth he had wrapped around it was bloodstained.

She waited until Mr Panirpour left. She reached out and handed her one tooman to Aqa Jafar. He took some tail, fat, skin and a little meat and a frozen bone from the counter, tossing them into the scales. Kowkab Soltan said: 'Aqa Jafar, don't give me that goddamn frozen meat from I don't know where. It's only good to be buried as fertiliser at the foot of trees.' Aqa Jafar grumbled that you get what you pay for: 'Do you expect me to give you Shishlik fillet for one tooman?' He wrapped the junk in a piece of newspaper and gave it to Kowkab Soltan … Would he have dared to if Haj Esmail had been alive?

What a panic overcame Kowkab Soltan! The panic was a disease in itself. She was afraid that she would remain as lonely as this all her life, that her son-in-law would never make peace with her and she would never see her daughter's face. Near the petrol station she slipped once and almost fell. The ice had turned the pavement into glass, and now the snow was covering the ice. Her other fear concerned the snow. She was afraid that the snow would keep falling for so long that she wouldn't be able to come out of her house, to go to Bagh-e Saba and poke around in the dairy shop, the butchers and the grocers of her daughter's neighbourhood and get some news about her. She was afraid that the snow would keep falling for so long that the doors of the houses would be buried under the snow, that the doors would not open, and that people would have to come and go through the rooftops. Her neighbours' houses had gable roofs, but her path would be so blocked that she would be imprisoned in her room, and then she would contract the disease that is said to have come from Japan; she would vomit so much that her body would be drained, and rot away all alone, without a nurse, in her room: die and rot away. Of course she wasn't scared of death. Freewheeling guys aren't scared of death, are they? She was scared of the snow and disease and loneliness and closed doors and the sulking of her son-in-law; but she wasn't scared of death, provided that she wouldn't suffer any pain, that is; provided that she wouldn't notice that she was dying; provided that she died in her sleep. Unlike Mrs Panirpour, she was no more scared of Inquisitor Angels, the first night in the grave and the Fifty-Thousand-Year-Long Day.

She had to make herself busy with something so as to not be scared of loneliness so much. How many more times could she knit, rip it up and knit again? She thought of beginning to make a patchwork quilt, searching in her bundles, gathering whatever pieces of fabric she had, sitting down and making a patchwork quilt. But for whom? Her daughter was scared of accepting anything from her. So for whom should she make it? In the first place, what and whom was she living for? To whom should she say hello to? Who remained that you could say hello to?

Heaven knew where in hell all those children had come from and poured into the alley, throwing snowballs and sliding on the ice and making slippery the passage of pedestrians. A snowball landed on her umbrella with a thud. She folded the umbrella and turned to swear. The faces of the children were red, and they were happily and joyfully sliding. She couldn't bring herself to swear. Hadn't she been a kid herself one day? Hadn't she had all the fun in the world? Hadn't she been a fireball? At the end of Ala'ei Street, the children had built a huge snowman. The snowman was a one-eyed man, and on his other eye they had tied a piece of black cloth with a black rubber band, and put a black *yarmulke* on his head. It was as though they were venting up their fury, for they were attacking with snowballs the snowman they had built themselves. They had struggled so hard that blood showed from under their cheeks. Their eyes sparkled. One of them was sliding on the ice, coming towards Kowkab Soltan. She was now under the drainpipe of a house, near her own. The boy kept sliding towards her, suddenly slipped, hit Kowkab Soltan, and both of them fell over; but the boy jumped to his feet and ran away. Kowkab Soltan was thrown to one side, her umbrella to another, and the meat – well, the junk meat – she had bought had dropped out of her hand and was scattered on the ice and snow. Kowkab Soltan didn't believe she could be so furious; it was as though she had been abandoned in a desolate desert on ice and snow. In accordance with the orders of the health insurance doctor, she started yelling:

'You sissies, you villains, you bastards! Have they closed the schools so that you give people hell? Heaven knows in what hell these bastards have hatched from their stinking eggs! Oh, folks, help me; this bastard killed me; threw me over and ran away. Must've broken an arm or leg. Someone take my arm and help me stand up. Do you only damn well know how to stick your nose up in the air, take fifty-tooman bills out of your pocket and buy two kilos of meat? Did you ever offer a goddamn bowl of yoghurt to your neighbour? May your mother perish in sorrow, may I receive the news of your death, may you never have peace in your life: you who have separated my child from me! Robabeh, where are you to see how ruined and abject has your mother become? Oh, Haj Esmail, what has become of you? I used to be full of smiles all the time; and look at me now. I wish to God no respectable person ever became abject. You godforsaken demons of kids, you have thousands of relatives when someone utters a word to you; but where are your relatives now …?'

A few passers-by approached her. A bearded young man with glasses bent over, took Kowkab Soltan by the arm and helped her up. He picked her prayer *chador* off the ground, shook the snow from it and put it on her head. A good-looking woman gathered the junk meat, wrapped it in the newspaper and handed it to her. The young man picked up her umbrella, held it above her head, put an arm round her and said: 'I'll take you home.' The good-looking woman said: 'If you think you've broken something let us take you to the clinic.'

Kowkab Soltan's heart was beating wildly, and her mouth tasted bitter. Nevertheless she smiled at the woman. Suddenly she thought that the young man was the son-in-law she had always wished to have but never did have; that the woman was her own daughter. Then she thought that all the people of the town were her relatives and associates, and this thought momentarily lifted her spirits. She said hello to everyone and promptly burst into tears, and now she was weeping as though Haj Esmail had gone missing only yesterday.

GOLI TARAQQI

The Shemiran Bus

The Line 70 bus leaves the station before we can catch it. My little daughter runs a few steps after it, but short of the bend she stops, disappointed. We wait for the next bus.

A sudden snow has started and a translucent haze swirls in the air. A nice silence has replaced the daily bustle of the city, and everywhere is white and calm. In the eight years we've been living in Paris this is the first time such a heavy snow has fallen.

Grandma's voice rings deep in my ears: 'The angels are housecleaning, they are dusting the clouds and sweeping the carpet of heavens.'

I think of Tehran's sunny winters, of the towering Alborz mountains under a bright ,clear sky and the hubbub of snow-sweepers on the rooftops, and of the poplars at the end of the garden, as white as lank old women. When I was a child, it was as though the snow would never stop once it started falling. Saturday, Sunday, Monday; I counted the days. Ten centimetres, twenty centimetres, half a metre of snow landed on the ground and the school was closed for a week.

What bliss it was! What unbelievable happiness! A whole week of staying in bed in the mornings, a whole week of playing in the alleys with a thousand and one male and female cousins; a whole week without the fear of seeing Mrs Superintendent or running into the bad-tempered maths teacher or reciting the Sharia book or writing homework; one whole week without memorising a long meaningless poem, or practicing calligraphy with a cane pen and black ink; released from the claws of the school and the lessons; seven days of freedom and playing!

How much fun was it when we had guests at home and the snow blocked the roads and all those who were in our house had to stay for two or three nights. Permanent guests of our house were:

- My thin, kind grandmother who used to pray day and night and beg of God for our happiness and health and longevity.

- Bibi Jan, my mother's old aunt whose ears could not hear any more and who was mentally disordered. She would take me for my brother and my brother for one of the cousins and the cousin for a neighbour and the neighbour for me.

- My lovely Auntie Azar who played leapfrog in the corridors with her naughty kids who ran up the doors and walls and trees worse than wild monkeys, or slid down on the handrail of the stairway.

- Uncle Ahmad Khan who was the kindest dentist in the world and could not force himself to extract anyone's tooth. His eyes were filled with tears whenever one of us cried.

- The older uncle, who was an artillery officer, who was scared of horses and frightened of guns and rifles. From the very beginning, he had taken off his military uniform, replaced it with a women's apron and stayed home. He made tasty jams and knitted colourful woollen jumpers.

— And finally, the fat, lazy Tooba Khanom who knew bizarre stories and had dealings with *djinns* and ghosts, knew witchcraft and performed juggling tricks for us.

All these people stayed in our house until the snow melted away. I just loved the crowded rooms, spread quilts next to each other on the carpet and tables heaped with all kinds of foodstuffs: sherbet decanters, bowls full of pomegranate seeds, plates of saffron pudding and pistachios and *sowhan* and *Isfahan gazz* and the delicious baklava that mother cooked.

What a joy was it when thousands of dizzying smells rose from the recesses of the house and swirled in the corridors: the smell of the tobacco of Grandmother's hookah, the lovely vapour of Bibi Jan's herbal potions and the scent of saffron on hot rice, together with the smell of cinnamon, cumin, fried onions and half-burnt kebabs on red-hot charcoal.

How I loved to go to sleep with the murmur of older people and their furtive giggles coming from the adjacent rooms. I would listen to the mellow sound of the younger uncle's *tar* and Auntie Azar's sweet singing and the 'tap-tap' of my mother's slippers on the stairs and then fall asleep. In the middle of the night I would wake up again. Seeing that the older ones were still awake and there was a lot of coming and going in the kitchen, and there was the clatter of the pans, I would go to sleep again, and my sleep was softer than the flight of a playful kite.

Today I'm again excited and happy at the sight of snow, just like when I was a kid. My daughter is also excited. She is spinning, dancing and making snowballs with her little hands, throwing them around. She frequently runs to the middle of the street, restlessly awaiting the Line 70 bus. Her restlessness reminds me of the beating of my own little heart when, everyday at sundown and after school, I worriedly stared at the end of the street, counting the minutes as I waited for my friend, Aziz Aqa.

I turn my face upwards. I open my mouth so that the snowflakes land on my tongue. What a nice taste and delicious smell they have, as though a thousand jasmine petals are falling from the gardens of the heavens. I feel as if my feet have left the ground and I'm floating in the air, as though I am in a glass bubble and a secret breath takes me back in time.

I take a look: I'm ten years old. At the junction near the school, I'm waiting for the Shemiran Bus. Our new house is at the other end of the world. We live beyond the hills and in the middle of arid lands. There is no other house around. Some nights, a jackal's howl is heard and my mother is scared. Hassan Aqa the cook is also scared and he spreads his bedroll in the corridor, behind the door of my father's bedroom. I like the house in the middle of nowhere, and I'm not scared of its big water reservoir, its swimming pool that is full of frogs and the dark shadows of its trees that resemble wicked men. At the far end of the garden and behind the box trees I have made a small hut for myself with old sheets. Noone can find me. I put my snacks under the bricks and bury under the earth, in fear of my mother, those homework sheets bearing a zero mark. The poplars are my playmates. Each of them has a name, and the taller ones are boys. Once back from school, I throw my bag aside and run to them. I tell them about all that I've done. I show them my drawings and I read out loud to them from my Persian textbook. Some of them are just asses and keep yawning. Some are wicked and don't listen to me. I kiss the ones that are my friends and stick my chewed-up chewing gum on their leaves. I beat up the ones that have talked behind my back and tie their branches together with a rope.

It's more than an hour by bus to Firuzkuhi School. My brother is older and is allowed to go to school alone. But I must put my hand in Hassan Aqa's hand and not take a single step without his permission. That's my mother's order. But I do as I wish, and I'll give him hell if he utters a word to my mother, because I know that the key to the upstairs storage room that's been lost is indeed in the lining of his jacket, and I know that when my mother's not home he steals handfuls of lentils and rice and beans from the sacks, putting them in a box behind the lavatory at the end of the garden, and takes them with him when he goes on leave. That's why we don't bother each other and are equal in terms of strength.

Hassan Aqa comes after me when the school ends at four in the afternoon, and we wait at the junction for the Shemiran Bus. Today it's snowing; the snowflakes are as big as saucers. Everywhere has turned completely white, and Hassan Aqa is standing by the wall like a blurred ghost. His face is like a transparent piece of cloud, one of those clouds that I see in the sky at nights and I know that they are the people of thousands of years ago. Some of them have crowns and beards and pass quickly on horseback. In the moon, if you look hard enough, there's a little kid sitting, with his legs folded onto his chest and his head on his knee and he's crying; but my dumb brother can't see it no matter how hard I try to show it to him. Mother is scared of the full moon and tells me not to stare at the stars. At times, from the violet depths of the sky a big dragon comes out and sinks into the Milky Way. Hassan Aqa screams when I tell him this. He hides his head under the quilt and prays loudly.

There's no sign of the Shemiran bus. I feel happy and slide on the snow in the middle of the street. I kick at the trees so that a flurry of snow falls on my head. Hassan Aqa is holding my bag and lunchbox under his arm and is shivering. A lifeless vapour comes out of his mouth. He's wearing father's old shoes. They're a few sizes too big for him. The shoe is gaping behind his heel, and the snow falls exactly into the gap. His hands are also small and he's wearing mother's gloves: ill-matched gloves, one ruby leather and the other black lace. Every New Year's Eve, father orders new jackets and shirts and shoes and socks and underwear to be bought for everyone. Hassan Aqa doesn't wear his new clothes. He puts them in a suitcase to take them with him to the village when he goes there in summer. Or he sells them and hides the money in the chimney in his room. I'm the only one who knows where his money is, but I don't touch it. I swear that I don't.

The sound of a bus engine is coming from far off. Hassan Aqa jumps with a start. Happily and anxiously, I look at this white box that approaches wobbling. I tell myself: if it flashes its headlights I'll get on; otherwise I'll wait for the next bus. Even if Hassan Aqa freezes from the cold and mother goes mad with anxiety and I die of hunger and fatigue. This is a secret noone knows about, noone. It's a secret between Aziz Aqa and me. Even Hassan Aqa doesn't know about it, and he doesn't understand why I sometimes don't get on the Shemiran bus (a bus that doesn't flash its headlights is not Aziz Aqa's) and run away and don't pay attention to his shouts and objections. Several times he's threatened to tell mother, and I have alluded to the key of the upstairs storage room that is in the lining of his jacket. That's why he doesn't bother me any more and doesn't pester me any more. The bus that flashes its headlights three times from far off is Aziz Aqa's. Every night before going to bed, instead of the prayer that mother has thought me, I repeat three times: 'I won't get on any bus but Aziz Aqa's.' This is a pact we've made – without saying it of course – until doomsday. Because I don't speak to my big friend who is even taller than my father and whose fearful face even the policemen are scared of. I don't dare speak to him.

The headlights of the bus that's approaching from the distance are turning on and off, and my heart's spinning like a top. I get on. Hassan Aqa goes before me; Aziz Aqa looks at me and answers my 'hello' with his swollen red eyes. His hair is greasy and frizzled. Hassan Aqa says he's had a six-month curl. His eyebrows are black and a thick moustache covers his mouth entirely. I sit on the seat behind him. Hassan Aqa goes to the rear of the bus where it's warmer, and is fast asleep almost as he sits down. There are no more than a handful of passengers, and most of them are dozing. It's quite a journey from the school to home, especially in winter when there's snow and the cars without chains slip in the street and the road is blocked. Some days Aziz Aqa is tired; he yawns widely and the smell of his mouth is more acrid than the smell of the tincture of iodine that mother puts on the wounds on my knee. My head is reeling and my bowels are growling. He looks at me in the mirror, making faces at me. He blows his cheeks. He tilts his nose and crosses his eyes. I put my hands on my mouth so that the passengers won't hear my laughter. I'm secretly dying with laughter. My friend looks like a ghoul and little kids are scared of him. He's got tattoos on his arms and on the top of his chest. There's a thick violet line between his ear and the other side of his neck. It's as though someone had tried to behead him.

Mother never rides a bus. She's got her own chauffeur and car; but she knows that there are ghouls like Aziz Aqa in the world, and she's worried about me. She doesn't like me to go to school by bus, but that's father's order and nothing can be done about it.

At the rear end of the bus, Hassan Aqa is fast asleep, squatting on the seat. A cold draught comes in through the broken window, and the passengers are freezing. Aziz Aqa takes out his jacket and puts it on my legs. It reeks with a stinking smell. I'd like the passengers to look at me, and I proudly run my hand over its greasy collar. My fingers get a strange smell, a smell that can't be found in our house, or in the houses of aunties and uncles. It's neither the smell of dogs or cats or cows or sheep. It's a smell that comes from the holes of an unknown world, the smell of all the bad deeds that oughtn't to be done and things that oughtn't to be known for a long time to come.

Mother's smell is different from all other smells. It's a smell that comes from foreign-made perfume and powder, from movie actors and fashion magazines and Lalehzar Street and the dance hall of the City Hall Café. Mother smells of the days to come, the smell of tomorrow and all the good things that are awaiting me.

With this jacket on my legs, I become a different person, someone who doesn't have to be clean and polite and a hard worker and a top student, tie a fluffy bow to her hair and say 'hello' and pay respects to everyone, and recite for strangers at parties a poem she has learnt at school and which she can't properly read by heart, to play for blabbing, bored relatives her first piano lesson, which is nothing but a repetition of flat *E, F, G, A, B, C,* and to take part in the 'Prettiest Child' contest and lose in it.

With Aziz Aqa's jacket on my legs, I become like him. I imagine that all my body is tattooed and half of my teeth are gold. I see myself wandering around in the alleys all alone and giggle and grumble like the daughters of Zahra the washerwoman. I'm riding on a bike, sitting behind the most handsome boy of the neighbourhood, going with him to see *Tarzan.*

When we reach Abshar Station, Aziz Aqa stops the bus. Most of the passengers get out to drink tea in the teahouse by the road. Hassan Aqa and I don't move. Before getting out, Aziz Aqa takes a small packet out of the bus's glove compartment and puts it in my lap. He looks at me in the mirror and winks. All his face is full of kindness, full of soft lines, like a cloth doll. My friend is the best ghoul in the world, and from his hands and legs, from the strange smell of his mouth, from his red eyes, from his old, greasy jacket something like a transparent vapour comes out that enshrouds me, and in this magical vapour I melt like a piece of snow and I feel so happy that I'd love to stay here and like this for thousands and thousands of years, like a stone statue, without growing up, without changing.

Today Aziz Aqa has bought me dried black cherries. Hassan Aqa calls me from the rear of the bus and asks what to do. I don't answer him. I hurriedly count my black cherries. The passengers are standing, sipping tea. Aziz Aqa swallows a few gulps of vodka from a bottle, then he goes behind the trees to urinate. I don't look. I look down and rapidly chew my black cherries. But I can see him in my head and my ears get hot.

We start again, going up to Vanak Square as slowly as an ant. At times the bus slides back. Other cars slip and stop right in the middle of the road in front of us. It's dark now and the whole world is white. Hassan Aqa is scared and calling me from the rear of the bus. I know that in a few minutes' time his teardrops will start rolling down. He's always ready to weep, and two or three times a day, with no good reason, his tears start streaming. Mother believes that Hassan Aqa's sorrows are like the cackle and cluck of hens and have no special reason. Father says that Hassan Aqa is a complete ass, and Hassan Aqa laughs because he loves to be an ass. Happily he removes the plates and looks at father's mouth, which is contentedly chewing pieces of kebab and is satisfied with his cooking.

The glass of the window beside me is broken, and a cold wind hits at one side of my face. My neck is stiff and my back is frozen with cold. Aziz Aqa is worriedly watching me in the mirror. He stops the bus, shoves a piece of newspaper and some old cloth into the hole and sits behind the wheel again. I know his silent language. He is anxious for me and he would rather I changed my seat. As if he is telling me with his eyes: 'Stand up, you spoilt little girl. You'll catch cold. Go to the rear of the bus. It's warmer there. I'm worried that you may fall sick.' And I answer him with my eyes: 'No. I won't move from here. This is my exclusive seat, and I won't let go of it.'

I love Aziz Aqa's anxiety. His motherly kindness shows the depth of his affection. I close my eyes and take an imaginary journey to the remote ages and the times of great kings, to the times when loyal warriors, in order to prove their honesty and devotion to the king, would walk barefoot on red-hot charcoal and fight the seven-headed dragon.

The bus isn't moving any more. The cold has replaced everything. The right half of my body is numb. I've got pins and needles in the tips of my toes, and I can't feel my feet. My head is as heavy as a mountain. As if it's been blown up. It's expanding and contracting. I'm frozen, and through my half-closed eyelids I can see shadows spinning out there in the snow. My nose is running and my eyes are burning. Suddenly I'm on fire. I feel hot, then I shiver and my teeth rattle from the cold. My tears fall rapidly. I can't do anything about it. Aziz Aqa dabs my cheeks with his rough fingers and laughs with his mouth shut. The students who know him say that all his teeth are gold. I don't believe them. I ask mother. She doesn't know; she doesn't know Aziz Aqa at all. But she doesn't like my question and angrily threatens to skin me alive if I look at bus drivers or speak to them. In mother's view, it's the bad guys and the roughnecks who have gold teeth; they're all thieves and murderers and do a thousand nasty things to little girls. I can't believe it though, and I feel pity when I see that mother sometimes becomes mean and tells lies and says that Auntie Azar is fat and ugly, and I am sad, for mother doesn't know many things. For example, she doesn't know most of the capital cities of the countries or the simple rules of arithmetic. Nevertheless, in my view she is the best and the most beautiful mother in the world, and at nights, before sleeping, I pretend to have stomach ache so that she would sit by my bed, and I'd like to confess what bad thoughts I have about her in my head. But mother is always after something. She is in a hurry and doesn't listen to me and she will punish me hard if she finds out that I've furtively listened to the talks between father and her.

Aziz Aqa is agitated by the snow and the cold. The bus won't move even a few metres no matter how he tries; it's as though we've lost our way in a white desert. I can hear Hassan Aqa's voice from the distance. He's groaning and loudly hiccupping with fear. I have a strange feeling too. The black cherries have filled my stomach, and I want to vomit. I'm hugging Aziz Aqa's jacket with both hands, and my head is reeling. I want to stand up, but my legs have no strength in them. I open my mouth but I can't make a sound. Everywhere is covered in snow: the entire city, all the world, and I've frozen under this frozen arch. It's years that I've remained frozen like this. It's only my eyes that are burning like a furnace of fire and my tears that are falling incessantly and my parched and bitter mouth, which is searching for water. Water, water, water …

A cool scented hand that smells of powder and cream is caressing my forehead. Someone's saying prayers into my ear and blowing at my face. Familiar faces are standing round my bed, and the large, sweet eyes of Auntie Azar are shining under the lamplight. I can smell Bibi Jan's potion. I know the softness of my clean blanket and sheets and I know that I'm in my bed and mother is beside me. A peaceful feeling fills my heart. I fall asleep and I dream that I'm riding on Aziz Aqa's shoulders and he is flying above the clouds like a flying carpet, taking me to watch faraway unknown cities. How I wish he opened his mouth and I could see his gold teeth. But what a pity! His lips are closed tight like the lid of a box full of jewels.

I'm seriously ill. Dr Kowsari comes to examine me every Thursday. My lungs make a rustling sound, and my fever rises at nights. He changes his prescription every time he comes, and I keep getting worse. I've become lean, yellow, deathlike, and my hair is coming lose. They bring me another doctor who coughs more than I do, and no chemist has his prescriptions.

Days and weeks pass like the wind. I've forgotten about school and the lessons. Grandmother sits by the bed and recites prayers and incantations below her breath. If I'm awake, she tells me stories and puts food in my mouth spoonful by spoonful. Every day I look through the window at the persimmon tree whose branches are bare and naked, and I keep counting the days until spring comes. Every day at four o'clock sharp, I see the Shemiran bus that's passing by the junction near the school, and Aziz Aqa, gloomy and lonely, looks at my empty place and drives by. Or perhaps he's forgotten me and gives to another girl the snack he kept in the glove compartment of his car for me. My heart burns with jealousy, and my coughs become faster. Apprehensively, mother calls Dr Kowsari and I hear father's voice ordering to have me prepared to be taken abroad.

This school year I will flunk; I'm crying, and Auntie Azar says that nothing's more important than my health. I wish summer would come sooner and the cherry tree would have leaves and fruits. In summer our house gets more crowded than any other time. Our family is a big clan, and I have tens of aunts and uncles and dozens of cousins. Father is the head of the clan and everyone obeys him. On Fridays, this clan has lunch in our house, and mother keeps most of the guests overnight. We all sleep together in the garden on the terrace. The kids sleep in a row next to one another and the elder ones under the poplars, on wooden beds and under mosquito nets. Father sleeps all alone in the arbour, on two sides of which there's a running stream whose swishing is heard till morning. Grandma sleeps with the kids and takes care of us. She puts a big glass of iced water above our pillows and a handful of jasmine petals under the pillows. She counts the kids and calls them by name one by one to make sure we're all there.

I love the living silence of the night. I can hear the heartbeat of the ripe fruits and the light breathing of fresh buds. Before going to sleep, I count the stars and look at the clouds that look like men. One of them looks like Aziz Aqa. He looks at me from far above and makes faces at me. My cousins keep murmuring, and grandma hits their feet with a long twig from where she is lying. The younger uncle snores and makes the dogs in the ruins bark. Tooba Khanom scratches herself with a screeching sound till morning. One of the kids keeps letting out a foul smell, and grandma rises angrily to find out who the perpetrator is. Everyone pretends to be fast asleep; noone dares to breathe.

Sleep, accompanied by the buzzing of mosquitoes and the twinkling of the stars, fills the eyes. Some nights it starts raining, and grandma covers us with a large, long, plastic sheet she always keeps handy. Under the thick cover, my cousin and I stick together like ants and listen to the clatter of the rain above us.

I've been imprisoned in the room since I fell ill, and everything scares me. Fear is everywhere, like an invisible man. Sometimes it opens the door, and in the afternoons, when everybody's drowsing, it comes for me. Sometimes it's behind the windowpane or hides itself under mother's skirt. This morning it was in the mirror, and it looked as if it was mocking me. It's fear that makes me cough. Mother doesn't trust Dr Kowsari any more and throws away his medication. Uncle Doctor sleeps in our house at nights. He's agreed with mother to take turns in giving me injections. Father says that foreign doctors are geniuses and cure the hardest diseases with the very first prescription. Auntie Azar looks at me with sad eyes and kisses my head and face as though she won't ever see me again. Hassan Aqa has an old postcard that shows a fat woman with blonde hair and a dress of velvet and lace. He says that this woman is the queen of Paris and that she doesn't believe in the Koran. Hassan Aqa is worried about mother and me and pleads to grandma to pray day and night to save us from this infidel queen. Mother is happily preparing suitcases for the trip. I know that fear is in Paris too and will follow us wherever we go. Grandma constantly prays and blows at my face. Tooba Khanom makes me drink a glass of boiled liver juice every evening. They have tied thousands of prayers round my neck and ankles, and the space under my pillow is stuffed full of small folded pieces of paper.

Every afternoon at four, I still think of the closing of the school and of the bus that's coming from far off; before reaching me, it disappears in a white haze like a half-forgotten dream.

I still repeat in my heart before going to sleep: 'I'll never get on any bus except Aziz Aqa's.' This is a pact we've made, and I'll be loyal to it till doomsday. I swear that I will. I close my eyes while swearing. I hold my breath, and my heart beats like a drum. I'm sure that Aziz Aqa hears the thump-thump of my heart and will answer me.

We'll depart in three days. Grandma is sitting by the window, passing a thread through jasmines, making necklaces and bracelets for me. Even Tooba Khanom, who always used to rock her buttocks and snap her fingers, isn't like before. Her eyes are full of tears, and she wipes her nose with the corner of her sleeve.

There's a knock on the door. I tell myself it must be a new doctor or one of the aunts. Thousands of people come to visit us, and the door is knocked upon hundreds of times a day.

Hassan Aqa comes into the room and stands by the door. He's bewildered and looks at mother in confusion. He wants to say something but doesn't dare. As usual he's hiccupping with fear. He points at someone or something outside the room, but no sound comes out of his mouth.

Mother is desperate and restless. She stands up and follows Hassan Aqa into the corridor. I can hear her voice: 'Who?'

I can't hear Hassan Aqa's answer. It's only mother's voice that rises higher and higher and worries everyone like a danger siren.

Grandma stands up and closes the window. She draws the blanket up to my chin.

Again I hear mother's voice: 'Bus driver?'

My heart's jumping out. I half-rise and sit up in bed.

Hassan Aqa's answer is like the baaing of a sheep that's about to be slaughtered.

Mother's shout swirls in my head: 'Who? What? Which bus?'

Nice Hassan Aqa is by now half-dead and stammering. I can hear mother's uproar; she wants to know how a ruffian driver has dared come to ask how her daughter is. She sends Hassan Aqa off to tell him that if he is seen around here again, she will have his leg bones shattered.

I push away the blanket. I jump out of the bed and run towards the corridor barefoot and in a thin dressing gown. Tooba Khanom tries to stop me. I push her aside and bite her hand. Astonished at my strange behaviour, mother orders me to go back immediately. In spite of all the threats, I make it running to father's study, which is at the end of the corridor. I get in and lock the door. The window looks onto the alley. I push the curtain aside. I climb a chair and see Aziz Aqa standing confused in the middle of the alley like a meek, embarrassed kid. He has a small packet in his hand. He's combed his dishevelled hair and buttoned his shirt up to his neck. He doesn't want his tattoo to show. I open the window. I call to him. He looks around and starts walking away. I call to him louder and wave my hand at him. He turns around. He lifts his head, and his glance falls on me. The same old kindness fills his face again. My tears are falling quickly and my words are unintelligible even for myself. From where he's standing, Aziz Aqa greets me with a nod of his head. God knows how happy he is. He comes forward. He comes towards me. He smiles, and with this smile something strange happens. His lips part:

his mouth is like a dark cave at the end of which a gold tooth, like Aladdin's lamp, is shining. I know that this magic lamp will give me whatever I ask for. I close my eyes and wish that I will become well again, that my coughing stops and fear will let go of me.

Once in Paris, we get a room at the Hotel Vagram; three days later a French doctor visits me and gives me a long prescription. I've been feeling better for a long time now, and I cough less frequently. Noone knows about my secret and the magic of the golden lamp; mother thinks my rapid recovery is because of the genius of the French doctor; but I know what and who has cured me. Every night in the dark and under the sheet, I run my hand against the imaginary Aladdin's lamp and repeat my constant prayer.

Our stay in Paris exceeds six months. Once back in Tehran, they change my school; my new school is no more than a few steps from home. I go there and come back on foot, but my heart sinks whenever I cross the street and my eyes look for the Shemiran Bus.

The years pass by rapidly, and I become a respectable young lady. Old buses are put out of service, replaced by shuttle cars driven by young drivers. But in spite of the passage of time, I've remained loyal to my great friend and my old pact. Whenever I feel sad or my heart feels heavy with sorrow or I have a problem, suddenly from beneath the memories of childhood appears my friend's magical mouth, and the glitter of that gold tooth shines like Venus in the darkness of my nights.

The Line 70 bus appears round the corner, proceeding slowly. A childish voice says deep in my ear: 'I'll never get on any bus except Aziz Aqa's.'

My daughter is walking ahead of me. She waves her hand for the bus driver; her eyes are full of playful, mysterious thoughts. Perhaps she also has a secret she won't tell me, just as I didn't tell anyone, neither my mother, nor Hassan Aqa, nor even the poplars at the far end of the garden.

MAHSID AMIRSHAHY

Khorramshahr-Tehran

Rezvan entered the station and dragged herself and her suitcase and her travel bag midway down the platform. Her footsteps echoed in the station. There was nobody there. Only at the end of the platform, a few porters and train conductors had gathered in a circle. The vacant place of the train was filled by a cold wind.

Rezvan put her baggage down; she felt like she was standing at the end of the world. She felt lost and forlorn. She was tired, she was regretful; fear of an unknown place and the fright of missing the train wouldn't let her relax. A feeling of vague anguish accompanied her like a fellow traveller. She was lonely and cold.

The overcoat had slipped away from her body and the wind penetrated her dress. Her feet had gone to sleep in her rubber boots.

She didn't notice when the station had become full. It was as if the crowd had suddenly boiled up from the ground and the walls and surroundings. The sounds blew life into the place. A few people were standing right behind Rezvan, and without looking at them, Rezvan felt that they were talking about her. She heard quiet whispers and loud collective laughter. She had no doubt that they were talking about her overcoat and boots. She knew that such thick winter clothes were unfamiliar for southerners. She was embarrassed that she was wearing an overcoat and boots but she was cold, it was cold, and the south was also cold.

She opened her travel bag. It was jam-packed – eyebrow pencil and lipstick and comb and hairpin and paper sheets and bills and keys and several lottery tickets and cigarette tobacco were all jumbled up inside. At the bottom of the bag, an old magazine lay half-open. Half of its pages were pressed against one another like a Chinese fan, and the corner of the other half was folded. She took out the magazine and smoothed it out and rolled it round and put it in a corner of the bag. She put her train ticket in the pocket of the bag and put the lottery cards in order and slid them inside the pages of the magazine. All of the cards belonged to weeks gone by, and she hoped that someday she would finally check them out to see if she had won.

She did up the buttons of her overcoat with frozen fingers. Without moving her head, she glanced to her right and left. There was noone to her right, and to her left a lonely boy was standing. The group that had been talking about her couldn't be seen.

Her boots had become heavy. She couldn't move. Cautiously she put her travel bag on her suitcase again and wrapped the overcoat around herself. She wanted to pull the collar up, but she was afraid of looking more ridiculous. She looked to her left again.

The boy standing there was looking at her. He was wearing an open-collared shirt, and a coarsely woven woollen jacket with leather elbow patches was on his shoulders. He had fine-woven, mustard-coloured pants and soft-soled suede shoes, without socks. He had his hands in his hip pockets and obviously the cold didn't bother him.

Rezvan shivered and wrapped the overcoat more tightly around her.

It was warm inside the compartment, cold and silent outside.

Along the railway tracks that were lying besides and on top of one another, a mixture of snow and mud was scattered. On the opposite bench, a couple had settled. The man was sitting and the woman had still her back to the door, moving the suitcases. The young boy was sitting next to Rezvan.

Rezvan's glance remained on the boy's eyes a moment more than she had intended to and then fell on her magazine.

The train sounded as if its wheels were square-shaped. The resonance of the sound was like the 'ting' of the string tool of cotton-beaters, and the heavy single thuds that hit the tracks in regular intervals were like the rhythm of the blacksmiths' hammer; a constant whistle howled in unison with other sounds too. The combination repeated a part of a song that sounded familiar in Rezvan's head.

There was still coming and going in the train's corridor. A few people opened the compartment door and peered inside and then closed the door and left. A young boy with a blue coat covered with black greasy stains, came in with a crate of Pepsi Cola and Canada Dry. Noone wanted anything, and so he left. For a while there was no movement but the movement of the train, and no sound but the sound of the train.

The woman sitting opposite Rezvan had her legs wide apart. Round, white flesh was bulging out above the elastic suspenders of her stockings. She was knitting. She had plump hands and three rings were imbedded in her fleshy fingers. She wasn't looking at what she was knitting. Her round, blue eyes were staring at Rezvan with a gaze like that of a dead fish. As soon as Rezvan's glance fell on her eyes, she asked, 'Are you from round here?'

Rezvan said, 'No.'

'Then you were here for vacation? So were we. But what a vacation! Oh, my dear lady! It was so cold we couldn't go anywhere. Did you manage to see much? We didn't. I never thought it might snow in these parts. Did you? They say Tehran's become so cold this year.' The woman paused a moment for breath.

Rezvan smiled in agreement and said under her breath, 'Yes.'

She wanted to read her magazine but was worried that the woman might get offended.

The woman put the knitting on her lap and offered a box of roasted nuts to Rezvan: 'Help yourself, it's homemade.'

Rezvan said, 'Thanks, I can't eat, I have an ulcer,' and laughed shyly.

As if sensing a foul smell, the woman wrinkled her nose and said, 'Oh – goodness me. Everyone you run into these days has an ulcer – what kind of a disease is this? My husband has an ulcer too. Are you on diet? The doctors have told Mahmoud he should eat something every three hours. He fasted last year, and you can't imagine what he went through. God forbid. I thought that – God forbid – he was a goner. This year I didn't let him fast any more. It's not possible, dear, with this ulcer and stuff. You can't do such things nowadays.'

Without lifting his glance from his newspaper, Mahmoud said, 'People have forgotten about being good Moslems, but I do have faith.'

The woman said, 'Times have changed. When in Rome, one's got to do as the Romans do. For example, do you think I can go to Mrs Colonel's house wearing a *chador*? Twenty years ago, yes, everyone was wearing a *chador*. Today women with *chadors* are called backward – aren't they? Of course they are.'

Looking at Rezvan, Mahmoud said, 'I swear by the holy Koran, the reason I made an 80,000-tooman loss last year was that I failed to fast. Now Parvin wouldn't believe it, but I do have faith.'

Parvin said, 'Oh, nonsense! Besides, what's money worth? May your body be healthy.' Then she turned to Rezvan, 'I always say good health comes before anything else. What's money good for? My older son – he's in Germany now – he's fifteen …'

Mahmoud interrupted her and said shyly, 'He's seventeen.'

Parvin looked at her husband with daggers in her eyes and said, 'What?' Then, without waiting for a reply, she said, 'Where was I? … Aha, my son had got sick – that was before he went to Germany

– I was willing to spend all my money for him to get well. Money's
nothing before good health, is it?'

Rezvan said, 'You're right.' She looked at the boy out of the
corner of her eye. The boy was smoking a cigarette and looking
at the ceiling of the compartment in boredom. Rezvan took her
cigarettes out of her bag.

Parvin said, 'My goodness! You shouldn't smoke with that ulcer.
Doctors have told my husband not to touch cigarettes. It's a whole
year that Mahmoud hasn't smoked. He used to smoke forty a day.'

Rezvan couldn't decide whether to strike the match or not.
The boy leant over the bench and held his lighter under Rezvan's
cigarette. Rezvan sucked at her cigarette with haste and hunger and
looked innocently at Parvin.

Parvin shot a poisonous look at the boy and said to Rezvan,
'You shouldn't smoke.'

Rezvan said, 'Yes – but, well … you know …' and giggled.

Parvin went on knitting more quickly for a few minutes. Then
she shook the gold watch that was buried in her wrist, held it to her
ear and said, 'This is so tiny that it doesn't show anything.'

Rezvan said, 'It's half-past one.'

Parvin immediately shoved the needles into the soft knitting
yarn and wound the woven part round the needles and the hobble
and stood up on her fat, short legs. 'Ah, how late! Let's get up
and go have some lunch. It's already late: that's why my stomach
was lurching. Did you take your medicine? Gosh, how hot is it in
here …'

The husband put his lamp-oil-coloured Shah Maqsood rosary
in his pocket, picked up his hat and followed the woman out of the
compartment.

The young man was still leaning against the corner of the bench
with half-closed eyes. Rezvan thought he was asleep, but when she
looked at him, he smiled. Rezvan got up and turned her back to the
boy and rearranged the things in her handbag without any reason.
She intended to take out her mirror and freshen up her makeup, but

she changed her mind. When she turned around, the boy wasn't in the compartment any more.

In the corridor a draught was blowing, and the movement of the train was more tangible. Rezvan wobbled past the compartments. In one of the compartments, a woman in a *chador* was sitting near the door with her milk-filled breast inside a baby's mouth. A few other women and men had put a saucepan in the middle and were speaking with filled mouths amid the munching sounds of others. A four- or five-year-old girl was pressing her face against the glass of a compartment door, watching the coming and going of passengers with astonished eyes. Rezvan smiled at the girl, and the girl hid behind the door, then she stuck her head out of the door and said, 'Miss! Miss!'

Rezvan opened the lavatory door. A mixture of water, lung phlegm and soap foam stood in the washbasin. The toilet was dirty and stinking. Rezvan rapidly closed the door and passed.

On the floor of another compartment a few men were sitting, playing with a deck of dirty old cards. One of them said, 'Stick!'

Another one said, 'Boy! We'd better back off. Mohammad is too lucky tonight.'

She passed several other crowded compartments. In this part, people and bundles and parcels were heaped up on top of one another. She asked someone, 'Excuse me, mister, where's the restaurant?'

The man pointed his hand in the opposite direction she was heading and said, 'At the other end of the train.'

Rezvan walked back all the way she had come. Her head was reeling.

The restaurant was still crowded. The smell of food had left little room for air. Rezvan didn't look at the faces, and sat at the first vacant table.

The food in the train's restaurant was too greasy, and the coffee tasted of lukewarm water loaded with chalk.

When she returned to her compartment, noone was there. She lay down.

A smell of oranges woke her up. She asked Parvin Khanom, 'Have we already passed Ahvaz?'

Parvin hurriedly swallowed the orange that was in her mouth and said, 'It's six; we've passed Andimeshk too.' Then with a tone more charged with adventure than affection, she asked, 'Did you want to get off?'

Rezvan said, 'No – I'm going to Tehran. Oh, how long I've slept!'

The boy wasn't in the compartment. Rezvan thought that perhaps he'd got off and the thought made her feel sad and she was surprised at having been sad. However, the boy's jacket and bag were in the compartment and Rezvan looked at them with excitement.

Parvin said, 'He came in and saw you lying down, then he left so that you'd be comfortable.'

'Who?' Rezvan asked indifferently.

'The young boy who's travelling with us.' And she smiled a meaningful smile.

Rezvan frowned and pressed her head against the window. The coldness of the glass made her body shiver.

Outside it was half-dark. The ghosts of trees and wires and telegraph poles passed alongside the train. Beyond them there was a scene that was as fixed and motionless as a postcard. The smoke that rose out of some of the chimneys stood in a certain spot, solid and thick. The constant movement of the train and the passing of poles and trees confused Rezvan. The train entered a tunnel, and for a few moments, there was nothing but darkness. Parvin's voice got lost among hollow sounds that were hitting the walls and the door and whirling around. All around the train, sounds were simmering and darkness was thickening. They came out of the tunnel.

Suddenly everything shrank to a tiny size in Rezvan's eyes. It seemed to her that the train was a series of matchboxes tied together. The far-off heights were like upside-down thimbles.

Parvin and her husband could be seen in the windowpane, which was a little distorting. Parvin's mouth was opening and closing but

Rezvan couldn't hear her voice. Mahmoud was playing with his rosary with rapid, nervous movements, nodding his head in tune with the movements of his wife's mouth. Both of them seemed to Rezvan to be dwarfs from fairytales. Everything seemed unreal and dreamlike to her. Her ties to the big, real world were entirely cut off. Tunnels consecutively rushed to welcome the train, and the train rolled and passed through the innards of the tunnels.

Outside the tunnels was also utterly dark. Rays from the train's light pierced a mere step into the dark and beyond that, a black wall stood against it.

Staring at the dark made Rezvan dizzier. Darkness was not monolithic and stationary; it undulated in waves like heavy slime. Before Rezvan's eyes, an infinite number of concentric circles were imprinted in the air and then vanished.

The circles were like interlocking doors, and beyond the last door a bright spot was shining. Rezvan passed through each single door, but her distance to the bright spot remained constant.

The train conductor came to check the tickets. Another man also came to put the beds in order.

Parvin was saying, 'We spoiled Manuchehr too much. Well, he's the youngest kid. And he knows well how to find his way into our hearts. He's such a mischievous scamp! That day – I mean before we left – he came to me and said … Parvin dear … Mahmoud, what did he say? He said something funny.'

The husband asked, 'Who?'

'Manuch – what did he tell me before we left? He said something funny. How could you forget it? It was so funny. Anyhow, he knows a thing or two. How many kids did you say you have?'

Rezvan didn't remember having said it before. She said, 'One daughter, one son.'

'Two? God save them. None of them were with you? They must be with your husband?'

Rezvan said, 'My son had to go to school. My daughter's married. She married this year.'

The train stopped in an unknown location. There was a sound of water passing through a clogged pipe.

Parvin said, 'Why did we stop? What's happened? It's not a station. Mahmoud, go have a look …'

The train started.

Mahmoud asked his wife, 'How long will we stop in Qom?'

Parvin said, 'We'll get to Qom unseasonably early.'

'Pilgrimage is never unseasonable – I just want to know for how long the train will stop there: if there'll be enough time to say prayers in the shrine or no.'

Parvin said, 'No, there's not enough time. We'll just stop there as long as the Qom passengers get off. Now get up and let's go have dinner – ask someone there if you don't believe me – and don't forget your medicine.'

The glittering light in the middle of the ceiling went out and the blue hue of the lamp over the bed settled on everything. Rezvan took off her boots and dress and lay down in the lower bed. She was neither asleep nor awake – she couldn't think; she could just feel. She felt that she was swinging in a point in space. Again it seemed to her that she was alone and at the end of the world, but she wasn't anxious any more.

Parvin's husband breathed loudly. Parvin couldn't be heard. It was too warm inside the compartment.

The door opened and the light from the corridor poured into Parvin's open mouth and the door closed and it seemed as though Parvin swallowed the light.

The boy stood by the door for a moment, then he fumbled towards the bed. He touched the bed cautiously. His hand touched Rezvan's arm and stayed there for a moment. Rezvan looked into the boy's face. At first she thought it was her son and then it seemed to her to be her daughter's husband. Her eyes smiled in a motherly manner. When she saw the lines on the boy's face more clearly, she recognized him and her anxious glance fixed on the boy's face.

The boy sat on the edge of the bed without removing his hand from Rezvan's arm. Rezvan's body stiffened. She dug her paw more deeply into the edge of the sheet and looked with terror at Parvin's bed and then at the boy. Her mind that had been foggy until then clarified and started to function. She knew that she was lying half-naked in bed and an unknown boy was sitting next to her.

She half-rose in bed. With one hand she pulled the sheet and the blanket further up on her chest and with her elbow she pushed the boy away from the edge of the bed.

The boy put his finger on Rezvan's lips and kneeled beside the bed. He gently slid his hand up and down Rezvan's arm a few times. Then he bent over and kissed the palm of Rezvan's hand a few times. Then he kissed her arm and forearm too. He put his head in Rezvan's palm. Rezvan abruptly pulled her hand away. Her head fell on the pillow and the boy's head landed on her belly. Rezvan struggled to push the boy's head away from her belly. The strap of her brassiere that had fallen on her arm came apart. The weight of the boy's head was pulling the sheet and the blanket down. Rezvan let go of the boy's head, trying to cover her bare breast, but it wasn't possible.

The vapour from the boy's mouth had condensed on her body. Rezvan abandoned her futile struggle and for a few moments kept breathing in time with the rhythm of the boy's breath. Figures and faces were dashing rapidly through her mind: the faces of her daughter and her son and her son-in-law, her neighbours, her relatives, Parvin, Mahmoud, the boy's face, the boy's young face.

The boy lifted his head and held Rezvan's face in his hands. Rezvan worriedly turned her face towards Parvin's bed again, and the boy turned her face back towards his own face with the pressure of his thumbs.

Rezvan thought, 'Will they know? Let them know! Let them know! Let them know!'

The boy changed the position of his head on Rezvan's bosom. Rezvan closed her eyes and threw all the images out of her mind, pulled her belly back inwards and thrust her chest up. Her heart filled the entire width of her chest. Her breathing was rapid and intermittent. She tried to imagine what she looked like when lying down.

Parvin uttered a few hurried and unintelligible words under her breath and rolled over. The bed creaked and the snoring of the husband stopped. He also rolled over and said, 'Parvin, are you asleep?'

Parvin was asleep and there was no answer.

Rezvan pushed away the boy in terror. The boy grabbed her hand firmly and rested his chin against her chest. A few moments later, the sound of Parvin and her husband's regular breathing was on track with the movements of the train.

Rezvan took in a deep breath and relaxed her flexed muscles. The boy let go of Rezvan's hand and accommodated himself on the edge of the bed quietly. Then he bent over and kissed her where her neck joined the shoulder and caressed her hair. Then he kissed the corner of her lip; then he kissed her entire lip.

The train came to a stop with a harsh jerk. The door of the next compartment opened and a voice asked, 'Are we there? Where's this place?'

The young boy's hair tickled Rezvan's face. Rezvan sucked her lips in, and the pins and needles in her face ran throughout her entire body. One of her hands was covering her bare breast and she dug the fingernails of the other hand into the boy's shoulder.

A loud voice from the corridor said, 'You're bound for Tehran? Go to sleep. We've still got a long way to go.'

The first voice persisted, 'Where are we now?'

There were footsteps in the corridor and someone said, 'Dorood, We're in Dorood.'

Several doors opened and closed and several shouts rose from inside and outside the train. The train started, first with uncertainty and then with resolve. The sound of the train became rhythmic and the same part of its song that was familiar for Rezvan started again.

Rezvan moved aside and made room for the boy, and he lay on his side. It seemed to Rezvan that a star circled around the bed and drew a blue ellipse and separated the bed from the rest of the space. It seemed to her that the bed was rolling inside the tunnels and passing through them independent of the train.

Rezvan's arms curled around the boy's neck and his forearm settled in the hollow of Rezvan's back. Their chests pressed against each other. The boy's body coiled around her body like the stem of a morning glory.

Only the unreal world was there. Rezvan didn't think of anything any more, she wasn't even wondering what she looked like lying there.

The compartment door opened and someone asked, 'Anyone for Araak? We'll be in Araak in ten minutes.' And the sentence was repeated several times like an echo until it reached the end of the corridor.

The boy was asleep, and the noise didn't wake him up. Rezvan's arm had gone to sleep under his body. She gently pulled out her arm and squeezed it. She felt pins and needles in her fingers, and they were shaking inadvertently.

Parvin was woken up by the noise. She sat up and her head hit the upper berth. She said, 'Mahmoud, get up, we're almost there.'

Her husband said, 'No, go back to sleep. It's only Araak. It's a long way to Tehran.'

Parvin rubbed her head and lay down grumbling because she had been woken up.

Rezvan shook the boy's shoulder and woke him up and pointed at the upper berth and smiled into his face. The boy looked at her sleepily for a moment, then pressed her to his chest. Rezvan pointed at Parvin and her husband and then again at the upper berth. As agile as a cat, the boy jumped out of Rezvan's bed and unto the upper berth.

Parvin was looking at Rezvan with her glassy eyes. Rezvan yawned and turned to the wall.

GOLI TARAQQI

A House in Heaven

It was a bad summer: hot, without water, without electricity. There was war and fear and darkness.

Confused, baffled and restless, like someone thrown into the depths of a chaotic dream, he grabbed the hands of his wife and kids and hastily left the country, without thinking, without knowing what kind of future awaited him. He didn't want to be wise and cautious and farsighted. He didn't want to consult with anyone, with those who were more experienced than him, those who were scared of any displacement and change, or believed in the soil and tradition and roots, whose staying was based on a moral decision.

Massoud D. hated the war and was scared of death. Nocturnal worries had drained him of all strength and patience, and a painful early-morning anxiety kept disturbing him. He had to leave, he had to escape and reside somewhere safe, somewhere far away from bustle and bombs and explosions, far away from the possibility of death ... He prepared everything furtively and in a flash. He put his belongings on sale and sold his house for peanuts to the very first customer. He obtained a visa, packed his luggage. It was just before leaving that, like a man in fever, his eyes fell on his mother and his knees faltered. He asked himself what would happen to her. Out of pain and desperation, his bowels twisted so terribly that for a moment he forgot about the war and death and decided to stay.

Mahin Banoo had all this time looked at him without questioning or objecting or commenting. She had seen her belongings go on sale and hadn't said a thing. She had seen strangers wandering in her house and she hadn't uttered a word. She had kept sitting by the wall in a corner, on the large Tabriz carpet – a relic of her ancestors – pitifully running her hand over its velvet flowers and gold-coloured figures: a residue of bygone days. The last touch of her fingertips on that old familiar object was like touching a lukewarm body in its last moments of life. And she had grabbed the tassels of the tablecloth to hold it for a moment. And her eyes had run after ceramic bowls with flower and bird motifs that were being passed by hands, and after the high-base Russian table lamps that had been sold. She had wanted to say, 'No, I won't let go of my cashmere bundles and my wedding mirror!' or to take one of those things and hide it away, but she hadn't said anything. She had kept sitting in a corner, quiet and invisible, full of wounds inside, witnessing the departure of the clock and the table and chairs and china plates and golden frames: like the sad journey of the children of an elderly mother to alien towns. She had realised that hard times were awaiting her and she had accepted it. She didn't have any complaints for her son. She had transferred her house deeds to him several years ago. They had agreed not to sell the house before her death, but it was an old pact, belonging to those times, before the Revolution and the war, before fear and trembling and the vagrancy of the kids. And Mahin Banoo didn't want anything but the well being and happiness of her son, or her daughter who had married an Englishman and didn't live in Tehran. For the sake of them she would give away – and had given away – the carpet she sat on, or her life, which was running out and which nobody wanted. Her children were in love with her too, and Massoud D. would have never thought of leaving her elderly mother and running away, or taking care of his own business while she was left stranded, homeless and penniless. However, amid the apprehension and chaos, amid the war and bombardments and the possibility of death, he had lost his mind and was no more responsible for his deeds and demands. This Mahin Banoo understood, and her silence, resignation and consent were borne out of this motherly understanding. Of course she had cried, she had cried a lot, furtively and away from others' eyes – in the night, in the dark and under the sheets, or in the day in the bathroom or behind the house's tall pine trees. She loved the cashmeres and carpets and old objects: legacies of her father and husband and the good old days of her youth. She had grown old with them, and there was an age-old bond between them. Her memories wandered in the rooms like thousands of images scattered in the air, and the footprints and fingerprints of her childhood remained on the cobblestones of the courtyard and the bricks of the wall. Other than this house, she had no place of her own, and now she could see that she no longer owned this place or any other; her feet rested on nothingness and she was suspended in the air. She wished she could duck her head and go away and disappear, like ailing or dying cats do. But she could see that she was lively and alive and not yet ready to die. Her elderliness was imposed on her by others. It was their ruthless glances and unfair judgments that determined her age and hit her in the face with the passage of years. She had a young vision of herself: an image reflected in old mirrors, in the happy memories of bygone days. Her heart beat fast and her eyes ran after things. She was awaiting the future; she was waiting for spring and summer. She had a thousand dreams, for herself, and for her kids, grandchildren and grand grandchildren. Seventy-four, seventy-six or more? These were calculations other people made, those who tried to estimate the dates of his marriage and birth. Mahin Banoo had not passed the fortieth mark. This only she knew and felt and believed. And now, without a status and a place, she didn't know on which moment of time she had fallen: who was she, where was she and what should she do. She had become something of a wasteland, out of the cosmic order of systems, like a fallen star, exiled to the disturbed isolation of the heavens. She wished that she had not been and had not become. Death was at a distance from her. Her feet longed for the earth. Her body grasped the particles of light and warmth, and her thoughts, with a thousand invisible strings, were tied to the corners and margins of a sweet life.

It was decided that Mahin Banoo would stay with her sister for several weeks or more (maybe even two or three months) until Massoud D. settled in Paris, rented a house and found a job, put his life in order, and then, at the proper time and with peace of mind and a happy heart, sent for his mother. Her daughter was also thinking of her: despite her low income and high costs of living, she frequently called from London and invited her. Her English son-in-law was a kind man too, and he was ready to accommodate his mother-in-law. However, they had to wait. Everything would finally be all right, maybe even better than before. Mahin Banoo was patient and wise, and her kids were indebted to her inherent intelligence.

The first two weeks passed a little hard; moving houses was not easy and Mahin Banoo was not accustomed to sleeping in other people's homes. She was addicted to her own room and bed and pillow; addicted to the sounds coming from the alley and the coming and going of her old neighbours; even addicted to the kitchen's stale smell and to the familiar moisture of the upper-floor staircase, and of course to the scent of the ivy outside her window and the eternal presence of those four tall poplars, the same age as his father. Her sister was kind and hospitable, and her husband, Dr Yunes Khan, didn't bother anyone: he was a depressed, lonely man and was sorrowful of his children being away from him. All his seven children had left Iran after the Revolution. His elder son was a resident of Australia; it was impossible to get in touch with him. His two daughters (his beloved twins) were in America. The middle son was wandering between Singapore, Thailand and Japan, and the youngest son constantly changed his base. And one of the daughters (Dr Yunes Khan thought – he wasn't sure, his memory didn't function) had become a citizen of Canada or India or an unknown country. The two sisters were close to each other, and Massoud was not worried about them; his conscience was at rest; he knew that his mother was comfortable – and that was true. Nevertheless, the nocturnal bombardments and subsequently the downpour of damned missiles had made a big change in Dr Yunes Khan's quiet temper, he had become obsessed with bizarre thoughts and he unreasonably suspected everyone. He eavesdropped from behind closed doors. He searched his wife's handbag or his sister-in-law's suitcase. He hid away his worthless collection of junk and forgot where he had put things. He was sure that Mahin Banoo had taken his glasses and lighter. He told this to his wife and she protested and the couple quarrelled and Mahin Banoo, crouched behind the door and shrunken with shame, contorted and kept counting the days: she wanted to go abroad as soon as possible to settle down with her kids. At the same time, she pitied Dr Yunes Khan, knowing that his deeds were not intended or committed out of nastiness. Even the day when her finger was stuck in the door and her fingernail was torn out, or the night when her brother-in-law disturbed her bed and searched her pockets in search of his agate ring, she neither moaned nor objected nor complained. She told herself that all those moments would pass; she thanked God that her kids were healthy, and that she was alive and alert.

Finally it was the promised day. Mahin Banoo thought that she was dreaming; out of utmost happiness, tears were flowing down her face: she who hardly cried before others! She couldn't help it. She kept kissing her grandchildren all over, and didn't want to take a rest or go to bed, although she had been up all night: the airport, customs, the searching of her suitcases, the loss of her handbag, forgetting to take her glasses and medications, the pain in her legs, the sudden dizziness and that damn nausea in the airplane. Notwithstanding all that, if she had been left to herself she would have liked to spend the whole day talking and kissing her grandchildren and son and daughter-in-law, to walk in that mouse-hole of a flat, and excited and agitated, ask them a thousand irrelevant questions.

For the first two nights, with much insistence and force, they had Mahin Banoo sleep in the children's room; they spread a mattress in the living room for the kids, whispering secretly in their ears that grandmother had just arrived and was exhausted, pity on her. They would later change her place and the kids could have their room back.

Mahin Banoo was sad to see the children's dissatisfied silence and their frowning. She wanted to say something, but she was too embarrassed. And she didn't have the strength; her whole body was shivering with fatigue. She fell asleep as soon as she laid her head on the pillow. She fainted, but near dawn she woke up with a start. She felt as though a weight of iron was on her chest, and an intruding unknown feeling, a kind of shame and humiliation and guilt circulated in her body. She remembered the upset look on her grandchildren's faces, and the thought that she had usurped their room agitated and disturbed her; it was as though someone poked her, as if needles had been planted inside her mattress and pillow. She would rather have slept behind the door in the corridor or squatted in the corner of a chair by the wall, than occupy someone else's place. On the third day they changed her place, and Mahin Banoo could breathe in relief. They gave her a lightweight foam mattress; at nights she spread it in the living room and during the day hid it under the sofa. She had put her suitcases in a corner of the kitchen and she dragged her handbag around wherever she went. The doors of the wardrobes would not be closed for the swelling of clothes, and there were heaps of stuff under the chairs. There was no room to move about. Mahin Banoo had for a lifetime lived in a large house with sunlit rooms, the view of the sky and the sun and the garden and flowerbeds. Her room had wardrobes and chests; hundreds of trunks could be placed in the storage room upstairs and a truckload of stuff in the cellar. Well, this episode belonged to the past. Life had ups and downs, and to sleep in a corner of the living room wasn't altogether without fun; well, there was much noise down in the alley and the underground train which passed near there shook the windows. However, from the first moment, Mahin Banoo told herself that life abroad was like that, there was no reason to nag, and thank God that she was with her kids and her life was put into order.

Her grandchildren were happy with their life. They liked their school and had made friends with a handful of Arab and Portuguese classmates. Every now and then there was a party, and Mahin Banoo had to change her place. She picked up her bedding and looked for a quiet corner. Where? There were two bedrooms and a narrow longish kitchen and a tiny bathroom and a lavatory at its corner. It was impossible to sleep in the couple's bedroom, although her son had insisted and her kind daughter-in-law had no objection either. There was no space in the kid's bedroom: two beds attached to each other and a handful of books and shoes and tennis rackets and a football on the floor. It only left the kitchen. She had no complaints: how much room would Mahin Banoo occupy? She was the size of a kid; lean, delicate and frail, she could fit into the pantry or under the bed. A couple of nights she had slept in the bathtub and she had in fact managed to go to sleep. But her son abruptly protested, and forced her mother to sleep in his bed, next to his wife. It was the worst night in Mahin Banoo's life; she was so ashamed in front of her daughter-in-law. She was lying along the edge of the bed, at such a distance that she would fall if she stirred; she couldn't close her eyes. The sheet ate at her, and her whole body was quivering. She had curled herself up so much that she looked like a little ball; she would roll down to the far end of the room if you flicked her. Her daughter-in-law was tolerant for three or four nights, but then she calmly informed her husband that it was not appropriate to carry on like that. Although a calm and reasonable man, Massoud D. suddenly blew a gasket for no obvious reason; he shouted and everyone heard his shouting; the kids panicked and the husband and wife lambasted each other, saying things they had never said before. Mahin Banoo died and came alive again; she damned herself for having come there and disturbed the life of a family, and the same day she decided to leave. She packed her suitcase and put on her shoes and jacket. She sat on the chair in the corridor and waited; waiting for her heartbeat to subside, for her thoughts to come to order so that she would see where she could go. She would go back to Tehran. That was the best thing to do. She would go to her sister's house. Back to Dr Yunes Khan and his weirdo acts? No, impossible; she would go to her cousin's house. She had forgotten that the cousin had died a couple of months ago, however, and now she was crying for her. She would go to her male cousins, to her nephews (the nephews had moved to America). She would go to the graveyard, to hell; she would beg, become a housemaid, whatever. At least she would be in her own country. She could lie down and die. One thing was clear: she wouldn't stay here.

Fortunately her daughter Manijeh (who was called Maggie abroad) called from London and insisted that her mother board a plane and fly to her that very day, that very moment. It was of course not possible that very moment, but they took her to the airport the next week. Like a bird released from its cage, Mahin Banoo found a new soul. The plane was like a house: warm and protected. She had her seat, her own seat. It would have sufficed her if she were also given a seat on earth; a tiny place she would know was her own. She ate her meal with eagerness and she remembered Nanneh Khanom bringing the dinner tray for her – in those days she was someone: she had authority – and how she felt pity and how she cried when she heard that Nanneh Khanom's grandson had been martyred in the war and her son had been taken to the lunatic asylum. Everything would have been different if this had not happened. Massoud D. had planned to rent a small place for his mother and trust her with Nanneh Khanom. That would be the best solution for everyone: for himself as well as for her mother. But who had ever seen the future? A mortar shell chopped off the head of Nanneh Khanom's grandson, doing him in right away. A few people came from Sabzevar, and havoc ensued. People came from the Revolutionary Committee, from the Martyrs' Foundation, with congratulations and consolations. And Nanneh Khanom was taken back to her village, given a room and a monthly pension. And she was set to stay there. And all this had happened before Mahin Banoo went to her sister's house.

Maggie (formerly Manijeh) hugged her mother and pressed her with such love and longing that Mahin Banoo sighed, a sigh of pain and happiness. Her son-in-law also kissed her and squeezed her hand hard. David Oakley was a nice man; he had Jewish blood, and that was why he was so warm-hearted. Mahin Banoo had not been happy with her daughter marrying a Jewish Englishman. She had wished to have a Moslem, Iranian son-in-law. She hadn't said anything though; she didn't interfere with he children's affairs. But at the bottom of her heart she had felt sad, until the day she saw the healthy face and wide, sincere eyes of David Oakley, and a heavy load was lifted off her chest. She held his manly arm, laughed, and she only just then realised how frail and little she was; her head stood lower than her son-in-law's waistline; she was like a chicken, no more than forty kilos – maybe less – with hollow bones and legs as narrow as pencils.

It was raining and cold. David Oakley had a car; he put the suitcases in the boot and cheerfully patted Mahin Banoo's delicate shoulder. Maggie sat next to her mother and rested her head on her painful shoulder. She whispered in her ear that she would never let her go back to Paris or Tehran, and Mahin Banoo's heart melted at all that kindness. She closed her eyes and fell asleep and didn't dream.

The flat of Maggie and David Oakley was on the fourth floor – no elevator. Tired and dizzy, Mahin Banoo was staggering. David Oakley lifted his mother-in-law, who was as light as a feather, and Mahin Banoo screamed, became erect and stiff like a pencil, and remained that way. Maggie laughed. David Oakley was in a good mood: he was holding his mother-in-law like a wooden doll under his arm and walking up the stairs. Mahin Banoo didn't move an eyelash. She couldn't believe it. She didn't know whether to laugh or to scream or to cry; such a thing had never happened to her. She didn't have a natural reaction or a ready response to accept or reject the situation; she thought that she wasn't herself. She felt that she had turned into an object, a broom or a chair bought from the market, and being a broom was a fresh experience, with its own particular world.

Maggie's flat was smaller than her brother's; it didn't have more than one bedroom. They had no kids. Still, they had a dog; fluffy and big; as big as Mahin Banoo. David Oakley was reasonable and logical, and he had reasons and principles for whatever he did. He wasn't emotional; he used his brain. He couldn't afford to beat around the bush. It was agreed that Mahin Banoo would sleep on the sofa in the living room. And when the couple had guests, she would lie in their bed – asleep or awake – and keep waiting. It wasn't a favourable solution, but what else could be done? Mahin Banoo had no complaints, no complaints whatsoever; and even if she did, she knew that it wasn't the right time to utter it. This made life easier for everybody.

David Oakley was a teacher. He taught economics, and he carefully wrote down all the expenses of the house. Fortunately Mahin Banoo was no bigger than a chicken, and she tried to eat less than a household hen. Maggie went to the university. She studied accounting. The couple left in the morning and returned in the evening, exhausted. They were hardly in the mood to speak, and if they did speak, it was about high prices and the cost of living. Mahin Banoo had no savings of her own. The very first day, with much insistence and begging, she had forced her daughter to sell her ruby ring and earrings. Maggie had said, 'No, impossible!' Her husband had said, 'Nothing wrong with it.' And Maggie had cried. First she had said 'no', but then she had accepted – of course reluctantly and with her husband's recommendation.

Mahin Banoo had learned to talk to herself. She didn't understand her son-in-law's language, and Maggie had to speak with her husband in English or not speak at all. They ate their dinner in silence. Maggie reviewed her lessons and David Oakley read the newspaper; all the pages, front and back. All three sat down and watched television; scientific and cultural programmes and chat shows and debates. Mahin Banoo stared, gazed, without seeing or understanding anything. She was immersed in her own memories, in another place and time. During the days she was alone. She cleaned the house and put it in order. She tampered with the two flowerpots on the windowsill, and watched the endless rain and the city's dull sky for hours on end. She was scared of David Oakley's dog, and most of the time she stayed in bed until her daughter returned. Sometimes she went out – if the weather allowed. She sat down on a bench in the park facing the block and shivered. It was a hard winter, and she finally caught cold. First her throat swelled and then her chest got infected. What coughing! It was as if she would cough out her entrails. Worse than all was the sound of her coughing, which prevented the next-door neighbour from sleeping; he banged his fist on the wall and Mahin Banoo hid her head under the pillow. She shoved the corner of the sheet into her mouth and held her breath.

Everything changed once spring came. A few rays of light appeared from behind the clouds, and the hearts were opened up. David Oakley took three days off and took her wife and mother-in-law for sightseeing and recreation. All of them enjoyed it greatly. Maggie bought medications and pills and syrups for her mother and Mahin Banoo even put on some two kilos of weight and thanked God from the bottom of her heart. But she had hardly finished thanking when the tide turned again. It was early summer; David Oakley used to spend two months of summer with his aunt in the mountains. It was impossible to take Mahin Banoo there. And during those two months they rented out the house to help with the expenses: it was understandable, particularly since the mother-in-law had brought extra expenses with her and they needed some extra income. They decided to send Mahin Banoo to her son in Paris. They made the decision abruptly. Without speaking to

Massoud D., they put Mahin Banoo on the plane and informed Massoud D. that his mother was on her way. It was the wrong time, and although glad to see his mother, Massoud D. couldn't keep her at that particular point in time. Any other time she would have been welcome, except for that time; she must understand. He said that it was impossible. It was summer time and the whole family was going to the South of France. They didn't have the money to stay in a hotel or rent a seaside bungalow; so they would have to live in a tent. They would sleep by the stream in the desert. Well, not in the desert: in the woods or on the plain. What was the difference? It was simply impossible to take Mahin Banoo with them. The sister and brother argued. David Oakley had several solutions. They brainstormed, and it was finally agreed to return Mahin Banoo to London and make arrangements so that she would stay there.

Although they tried to talk in whispers and speak quietly, Mahin Banoo could hear their talks and arguments, and pressed the tip of her toes to the ground so that maybe a hole would open up and swallow her. She saw that she was being passed around like a useless object; her head was reeling.

Firuzeh Khanom was one of Maggie's friends. She had a small laundry, which provided her means of living. They asked for her help. Firuzeh Khanom was good-humoured and witty. She said that she lived in a tiny room herself, and that she had no room for a guest. However, behind the laundry there was a vacant storage room; it didn't have any windows, but was warm and protected. David Oakley agreed. Maggie was unhappy, but she didn't have much of a choice and so she kept quiet. Mahin Banoo agreed too: she wanted the whole business to come to a close quickly.

The room behind the laundry was damp and dark, and the first night Mahin Banoo cried till morning, asked God to help her die. She asked herself what had attached her so much to life, and where on earth her strength came from. And she saw that it was all because of her love for her kids, and she made a vow to God to take that love out of her heart so that she would be relieved.

Firuzeh Khanom was a nice woman. She was a match for ten men. She had a husband who lived in Tehran; one of those melancholic, opium-addict husbands. Once a year, at his wife's expense, he went abroad, moaned and groaned, complained hither and yon: a depressed, hollow, good-for-nothing man. In the old days, he had been a respectable person, or so he thought. Educated: into books and translation. He had been devastated with the first blow: disturbed and disappointed. Firuzeh Khanom was a lion of a woman. She couldn't stand howls and moans and groans. She had sent her kids to England. She had gone to London herself and started a business. She was also manly and helpful: she helped those around her — if they deserved it. As soon as she set her eyes on Mahin Banoo — the sweet face, the sad amber-coloured eyes — she was fascinated by her. She did her shopping for her; she had her sit by the machines in the laundry, brought her Persian books and newspapers to read and kept her busy.

Karim Khan, Mahin Banoo's brother, lived in Canada. He had money and a house, and even a garden with a few birds and rabbits. He heard, through word of mouth, about the jarring state of his sister, and he blew his top. He was so offended that he wrote to his niece and nephew, and insulted and humiliated them (maybe he went a little too far, but he couldn't help it). He ordered them to arrange for his sister's move. He had an acquaintance in the Canadian Embassy who helped him obtain a visa for Mahin Banoo. He sent her the air ticket, and when Massoud D. or Maggie tried to interfere, he phoned them and yelled at both. And since he was the senior member of the family, they both backed off.

It was in the beginning of winter when Mahin Banoo departed for Canada. She was glad that she was again between heaven and earth, that this was the longest route, what a joy! She sat by the window and her gaze remained fixed on the transparent light outside. Her seat was soft and warm and that was what she wanted: a corner immune from other people's aggression. She had a fever, and the sunshine behind the window gave her great pleasure. One moment she would fall asleep, her head dropped onto her chest, and then she would come to again; her eyelids opened halfway and her glance travelled to the end of the horizon, to the end of that vast expanse, expanded till eternity. Beneath her feet was a plain of white clouds – bright, light, immaculate, like a providential dream, the dream of the elect carefree angels.

Someone said something into her ear; it was the passenger sitting next to her. She didn't hear it. She declined the food tray and turned her head away. She pressed her face against the windowpane and inhaled the sunlight with her fascinated eyes. She felt that a thousand tiny stars were twinkling in between her thoughts, and a lamp was lit inside of her.

The blue sky was a monolith, without a speck of cloud, without an irrelevant impulse or inappropriate undulation, reaching as far as the last frontier of imagination, as far as the origin of things, beyond commonplace forms and current scales. Mahin Banoo saw herself at the age of twelve, playing in the garden in Damavand; it was snowing and her fingertips were numb with the touch of those hollow frozen feathers. She was watching the mind-boggling falling of snow, looking at the grey end of the horizon, and she felt as though her feet had lifted off the ground and she was flying towards the sky. She loved this game; she didn't forget it even when she grew old. She would sit by the window and Nanneh Khanom brought her tea and *nabaat*.[1] They both kept staring, like *jinn*-haunted people, at the monotonous whiteness of the outside, and very slowly drifted into sleep. She would wake up in the middle of the night; she knew that the snow was still falling, and she listened. The whole city was sleeping, frozen, beneath a white cover, like a house with nobody in it, with its furniture hidden under clean sheets. No sound could be heard except the magical silence of the atmosphere, overflowing with nothingness, with the silent presence of God.

All through the journey, in fever and drenched in sweat but joyful, she was sitting by the window and she was so intoxicated and

---

1.　Crystallised sugar.

fascinated by what was outside that she couldn't remember where she was or who she was. She was drowsing. She was dreaming. She kept coming back to herself. She looked. She remembered her memories and drifted again. She was spinning. She was in the snow. In the centre of the sky. She was sliding. She was everywhere, in different times; in a single moment she could see thousands of images of herself, scattered in space, or a column of different Mahin Banoos, some old, some as a child and young, in this life and in other epochs. A woman raised to the power of infinity, women tied to each other in a chain of eternal return. It was the first time that she wasn't thinking of her children or of people on earth: of the large Tabriz carpet or her cashmeres, of her house in Pahlavi Avenue or of her earthly memories.

She was above the clouds and the huge expanse was very slowly entering her body and settling down at the bottom of her soul, like the pleasant warmth of autumn, moist and languid, and making a cocoon, weaving a web around her and spreading an umbrella over her. It was as though she was in the womb of the cosmos, protected and immune, beyond time.

Karim Khan was impatiently awaiting her sister's arrival. He had decided to keep her with himself, and he was embarrassed at the carelessness of his niece and nephew. He burst out crying when he set eyes on Mahin Banoo; he too was full of grief and torn apart from his relations. A thousand times a day he longed to go back to his homeland and then he discouraged himself. Seeing her sister, old, broken and vagrant, renewed his grief. He told himself 'to hell with exile' and for a moment it crossed his mind to go back. He had a garden and real estate of his own; he would go back to his home and his life and he would live with Mahin Banoo. They were close to each other; they had grown up together, and the age gap between them was not large. He was shocked to see Mahin Banoo. How thin and pale and confused she was. She kept looking, but she didn't see anything. Her mind was in disarray. He was shocked when he held her hand; it was just a piece of hot bone. He spoke to her; she didn't hear, she didn't understand. She gave nonsensical answers. Agitated and devastated, he hugged his sister and kissed her all over the face. He felt his own old age and a pain wrung his heart.

When they reached home, he put Mahin Banoo to rest in a large bed and called a doctor. He telephoned her children and told them about their mother's state. He explained that it was all about the fatigue from travelling and sleeplessness and high blood pressure, that it wasn't anything serious; that there was no reason to worry; and he took to looking after his sister. He was excited and overwhelmed with joy and he had so much to say he didn't know where to begin. He spoke of the past, of childhood days, of yesterday and the day before, of himself and his sudden decision to go back to his homeland. He was laughing, he was joyous. He couldn't believe that he had decided to return, and he owed his sudden happiness to his sister. He couldn't understand how the thought had struck his mind. Maybe he had been shocked by the sight of his sister's dazed face and her wandering presence. He looked at Mahin Banoo's staring eyes, which seemed to be devoid of any familiar memories and reasonable thoughts, and he was scared. He could see the meaning of exile in her, and it shook his heart to the very bottom. He had just realised how lonely and isolated he was; that there was nothing beneath his feet and that he had just a transient and temporary presence, like an alien traveller in a cold and sad railway station. He held Mahin Banoo's hand and kissed it. He told her that her vagrancy and homelessness had come to an end; that they would return as soon as she recovered; and Mahin Banoo closed her eyes; she saw herself sitting by the airplane window and the blue expanse calling to her. She fell asleep and again dreamt of the sky that was flowing like a fluid sea towards the bright regions of being, and she couldn't know how many days or dozens of days she had been sleeping. She felt thirsty; she stood up; her legs were trembling. Karim Khan wasn't home. She looked around. She couldn't remember where she was. A soft light was pouring in through the lace curtain of the window. She went forward. She put her hand on the back of the chair. She paused to take a breath. She took a couple of steps and she felt as if she had moved mountains; sweat was running down her face. With a trembling hand, she pulled the curtain to one side. It was snowing. She listened: the same old inviting silence. Nanneh Khanom had brought her tea and *nabaat*. She was standing by the door, crying. Her grandson had been martyred. She was leaving for Sabzevar. She said, 'Wait, Nanneh Khanom, I want to give you some money for the trip.' And put her hand on the door handle. She was tired; she wished to sit down. She was looking for her seat. The airhostess was checking her ticket. A gust of cold wind hit her face. She shivered. It was snowing; snowflakes were heavy, as large as saucers. She stepped forward. Her foot slipped. It was a cold airplane. She couldn't find her seat. She stepped further forward. A cold road stretched ahead of her. The snow went into her eyes. Mount Damavand, towering, unwavering and glorious, was looking at her from far off. It was as magnificent as her father, when he stood to pray and the wind blew under his cloak and it seemed to her that his head touched the sky and his feet were rooted in the ground. How nice a time it was when she lived near this mountain that scraped the firmament, this mysterious awesome height, this man standing between two marble columns of the terrace at high noon, with his shadow stretched to the end of the world. How joyful it was when she crawled underneath his cloak and climbed over his back, over the highest peak in the world, beyond the earth and the small clay houses and the men the size of ants, feeble and meagre. She could see the same picture when she looked out of the airplane window, and it seemed to her as if she was again riding on her father's shoulders and nobody could reach her, neither her mother who reprimanded and blamed her, nor the bad-tempered arithmetic teacher who told of eternal multiplications and divisions, neither the policeman down the alley who twisted her ear, nor her husband who restricted and bullied her, neither her kids who were hanging on her, devouring her flesh and blood with an animal pleasure, nor others who set moral criteria and historical philosophies for her and

filled her skull with the crushing weight of words and estimated the
borders of her sight and limits of her intelligence with their short
geometrical rulers and miserable mathematical scales.

Someone was calling to her; maybe it was beyond Mount
Damavand. She ran, she turned around, she turned into a street
on her left, filled with snow, she felt hot, burning, she took off her
jacket, undid the buttons of her dress and turned her face to the
sky. She remembered the childhood game and laughed. The snow
went into her mouth. It was delicious. She looked, she looked, she
looked. She kept staring, without blinking; her feet lifted off the
ground; snowflakes were transfixed in the middle of the air and she
was ascending; she was in the sky, over the clouds; she saw Mount
Damavand; it was down under her feet, and on its peak was placed
a large comfortable armchair of walnut wood and red velvet – the
same chair that used to be in her father's study. The airhostess guided
her to her seat, her exclusive seat! She sat down. She was the size
of a little kid and she was lost in the chair. She wrapped her father's
cloak round her and pressed her face against the windowpane. The
sky was a monolithic blue; limpid like a spring of light. And the
huge expanse, vast and generous and magnanimous, was looking at
her. She listened: there were no sounds but the silence of the falling
snow and the sweet quiet of death.

Massoud D. blamed his sister and considered her guilty. His
sister complained about Uncle Karim. David Oakley said that such
events happened all the time, and since he taught at the university,
he spoke of the law of cause and effect and the rules of history and
economy. Firouzeh Khanom grieved and then forgot. Others also
forced themselves not to forget Mahin Banoo's story, but they did.
With all those problems and all that misery and work and fatigue,
amid war and exile, how was it possible to retain one's memory?
And this Mahin Banoo understood well. Thank God she was an
intelligent woman.

MIHAN BAHRAMI

Garden of Sorrow

Our alley was narrow and the thatched façades of its houses had a monolithic village hue. At a bend midway down the alley, a corpulent acacia tree hung over the water stream, looking at its own branches and twigs.

Our house was at the end of the alley, and a little farther, the alley came to a dead-end at a large, wide gate. Through the planks of the gate, which were decked with spikes, one could look at a vast garden, which the residents of the alley called the 'alley-end garden'.

During the days, other kids and I drew hopscotch grids in front of the garden's gate, played with pebbles and rope-danced. But when the games ended and the kids went home, I climbed to the rooftop through stairs in the house's porch and adjacent to the garden's wall, and furtively watched the garden.

The garden was rectangular and vast; from its gate stretched a narrow street paved with gravel, beyond it there were orderly furrows of vegetables framed by rows of blue cabbage. In between the furrows, in rectangular patches of land, camomile and coriander sprouts were planted, and the white flowers of camomile, intermingled with wild violet morning glories, were like petals scattered over the surface of calm waters by the spring breeze. Beyond the vegetable furrows was a row of poplars.

The silence of the garden was only broken by the cawing of crows nesting in these trees, and at noon by the jingle of the bells of mules bringing fertiliser. At such times, the monotonous song of crickets from coriander bushes combined with the brass tune of the bells of mules to form a joyful, sleepy melody, which, especially in spring afternoons, made me dizzy; the cob of the rooftop burned my bare toes; I never went down until there was some uproar and I was called and threatened. At noontime the garden was more beautiful than at any other time. The gardeners left for lunch and sparrows swarmed the trees and their manic chirping stirred an uproar.

Thousands and thousands of luminous golden stars shot from the sparkles of diehard dewdrops and from the tips of buds of plants, and the trees and flowers fell asleep under the soft umbrella of the singing of beetles and crickets.

The garden's trees were acquainted with me; I had divided them into families: opposite the garden gate was a thick old plane that would be grandfather to all the others, and then in the row of poplars there was a family with three kids: two tall and lean trees that easily swung – these would be the sons – and a shorter, bushier one that would make the little daughter. There were also a few elms at the eastern end of the wall; single and without mates, with a dark green hue; they all looked to me like the old maid who lived a few houses down from ours and was on fighting terms with everyone save the kids.

I was so attached to the trees and vegetable furrows and the sound of mules' bells that I could feel the slightest change in them, and if I closed my eyes I could see them in my mind as lively and undulating and green as they were. If I heard the bells from far off

I would distinguish whether the mules were loaded or not, coming or going, and if I didn't go up to the rooftop every day it was as if I had lost something; I imagined that an unknown being was awaiting me in the garden, and this was not an irrelevant conjecture, for when I had enough of watching the garden and wanted to go down my glance was for no reason drawn to the western end.

There was a big dark mulberry tree there, which looked as if it had grown at the top of a hill. Its bark was halfway covered by its own rotten leaves and the garbage and fertilizer buried around it. Down the hill, opposite the mulberry tree, two empty dark sockets of the window of an old door, which was always closed, always looked like they were staring at you.

This place was called 'snake-haunted barn'.

My grandmother said, 'The landlord's snake is in the barn; in the past it has bitten every cow or donkey that was put into the barn; its old poison turned the animals into limestone.'

Bemoon Ali the gardener said, 'The snake is an infidel. And killing a snake – Moslem or infidel – brings bad luck; that's why the barn is abandoned.'

Some of the women said that on summer afternoons they had seen the snake twisting its wide body with its blotches and markings on the wet soil under the mulberry tree, sticking out its forked red tongue, panting and searching for water. Its mouth was so large that it could have swallowed a small head.

Old gardeners said, 'This is not a snake any more; it's become a dragon; if it comes too close you'll see that even its breath is venomous.'

It was because of those stories that I stared at the glassless holes in the old door with a stinging curiosity, looking into it with gruesome thoughts that came to my mind. I was scared and at the same time fascinated by the barn and the story of the snake. Even when watching the garden, I tried to make myself busy with butterflies and trees or Bemoon Ali's ginger kid goat that he tied to the *jujube* tree; but a strange attraction drew my glance to the mulberry tree and forced it into the darkness of the windows of the barn, and after staring at the darkness for a while, I saw ambiguous figures. Nevertheless, watching the garden had such an attraction that it filled my loneliest hours, which were usually from morning to afternoon.

But sunsets were something different altogether.

We spread a kilim on the rooftop next to the wall, sprinkled water on *rashti* straw mats and spread them under the bedrolls and brought the samovar onto the rooftop.

On the other side, in the opposite direction of the garden, beyond domed thatched roofs and Shah Abbas caravanserais, there was a multitude of pine trees of an old house, through the branches of which, the glistening tiled dome and minarets of the Shahzadeh were visible.

Beyond the dome and the minarets, on the purple-azure horizon, beneath a conspicuous star that appeared in the sky before all the others, was the brick arch of a roof on which a stork stood on a long leg and I never saw him with both claws on the ground.

From there came the ambiguous hum of the alley and the street, gradually dissolving with the coming of silence, and eventually joining the silence of the evening. At that moment the strokes of Shahzadeh's clock echoed onto the pine branches and the multicolour sparkle of the minarets' tiles, and immediately after that the deep, melancholic voice of the muezzin rose. What sunsets! There was the sound of grandmother's hookah gurgling and her lamenting voice praying, and the call to prayers was the best opportunity for the forgiveness of her sins. Wherever I happened to be, playing or on the rooftop, I could see her battered face nodding in response to the neighbours who said, 'Lady, sorrow will destroy you.' She would move the pipe of her hookah and dab with the corner of her headscarf the teardrop that lay at the corner of her eye.

How I wished I could grieve, pray and utter ambiguous words. But I despised smoking a hookah. I liked to sit down and watch the inside of the crystal hookah's water container, where she used to put a few red rose or Damascus rose petals. Two wooden dolls, swollen and darkened from the moisture of water, were tied to the bottom of the pipe. When she pulled on the pipe the dolls swirled in the water bubbles, as if they were running after the petals, and I died of laughter watching them turning somersaults. When there was not much water in the container sometimes a narrow strip of smoke came out of the pipe's hole and crawled in the space above the water surface and the dolls remained dazzled and motionless and I saw the ghoul of grandmother's stories growling through the hole in the hookah's neck, searching for the wooden dolls to swallow them in one go. I thought that if grandmother removed the neck of the hookah from the container, the ghoul would come into the room. Then I looked at my grandmother. Her face was tired and gloomy and I thought that I should look like her. I pursed my lips, sighed and swallowed my saliva, sometimes I squeezed my throat with my hand so that my saliva would go down uneasily, and I sobbed and tried to show grandmother that I was grieving just like her. But a moment later when she wrapped up the hookah business and left, I had already forgotten everything and I started turning somersaults and watching the upside-down dome and minarets. Sometimes I recited the poem on the death of Nassereddin Shah, which I had learned from grandmother:

> *Nassereddin, the just king*
> *And prime minister of the land*
> *Went on pilgrimage Friday*
> *Ladies of the harem became homeless*
> *Children of the harem became fatherless*
> *Less ... less ... less ...*

In time with the refrain I first clapped and next time hit my knees with my hands, and I remember that instead of 'prime minister' I used to say 'crime sinister' without paying attention to the meaning of the poem. I didn't pay attention to the meaning of anything at all; I just liked to sing and bounce; singing and bouncing had immense pleasure. When I was entirely exhausted, I lay on the mattress and busied myself watching the sky. The cool canvas smelled of the roof's thatch and moisture, making my body numb and inert.

Far away, thousands of stars shone, and over my head, in the blackness of the sky I saw the Mecca Way[1] and imagined that my father had gone on a trip along that path.

On midnights when I was woken up by the noise of fighting cats or the muffled struggle of couples sleeping in our vicinity, the bright circle of the moon was walking next to a big star on the limpid deep sea of the night, and a piece of cloud that had opened its mouth was crawling in a horrid way in its wake. The moon's face was sad and the mark of the sun's paw showed on it.

The day was another world, with much gambolling and a multitude of games; we drew grids with charcoal on the ground before the garden gate at the end of the alley, and our entire time was spent playing hopscotch and giving piggy-back rides to the winners, and how much humiliation we suffered when neighbours wiped off our black grid with their feet. Good and bad omen depended on a piece of chalk that we didn't have.

That morning it was my turn to play; as I had one foot up and was kicking the stone with the other, I saw grandmother come out of the porch. Although all my attention was grabbed by the movement of the stone and the borders of the grid, my glance fell on grandmother and her long body that looked a little arched, for she was wearing her formal dress: white, black-dotted *chador* and black stockings and red-lined Russian boots. She had tied the ends of her headscarf together so that her hair would not stick out. Her face was showing: she covered her face with the *chador* only when she left our alley; with the neighbours she practised no formalities. She didn't see me; she passed me by and went to one of the neighbouring women and exchanged pleasantries with her and then I heard her say:

----

1.   In Persian folklore the Milky Way galaxy was regarded as the road to Mecca.

'Yes dear, I told myself to go to his grave this Thursday evening and weep and get it off my chest. You know I can't do it at home ...'

The neighbouring woman said in a reproachful tone, 'What's the use of it all? Do you think he'll return? Whatever you want to do, you should do it for *her*.'

And I saw that she pointed in my direction. Without looking at me, grandmother said goodbye and left; the neighbouring woman grumbled to herself, 'After all this time, her wound is still fresh. May God give her patience. I've never seen anyone mourn so long for a son-in-law.'

At that time I couldn't properly understand the meaning of such remarks, but based on all that I'd seen, I found a new feeling in me, and maybe it was the first time that I seriously thought of my father. For a moment, everything ran away from me, but the shouts of the kids brought me back to myself. They picked the stone up from near my foot, yelling, 'You failed in square four, so you must give someone else a piggy-back four times, you failed ...'

For a while, I stood where I was, transfixed: So my father hasn't gone on a trip, he's dead, now I'm an orphan ...

I looked at the kids. Did they know?

Panic overwhelmed me. I don't know why I was panicked. I didn't see myself as an orphan in the least, for any orphan kid I had seen until then was shabby and poorly looking. For me, being an orphan meant being a beggar, the beggar kid who held out his hand to us and said, 'Please have mercy on this orphan!'

Among my playmates was a little boy whose father had fallen in a well and drowned. A big blue Aleppo boil under his eye hit you hard when you looked at him, his nose was always running and snot was smeared on a corner of his lip. My heart sank. I didn't want to have any resemblance to him at all. To my eye, he was a faulty creature and I harassed him adequately.

I was a beautiful kid; this everyone said. To me, my brand new shoes and beautiful dress were the best things in the world. I imagined that at nights, up over there, at the end of the sky, a place with mirror-work and a golden dome like the Shahzadeh shrine, there was sitting a god who saw me, remembered me, loved me and would return my father to me. Who could say that I had really heard those words?

Maybe my father had really gone to Karbala?

I was thinking of Karbala; it was the first time that Karbala became so important and even frightful for me.

'Is Karbala somewhere noone returns from once they go there?'

What journey? No, I was sure that my father would come back. But something in my heart evaporated; grandmother didn't seem the same to me as she had before. Her lying distanced me from her. I could no longer listen to her like I had before. Again I remembered the neighbouring woman: 'He'll never come back.'

I couldn't make myself accept that my father wouldn't come back, even if he were dead. I convinced myself that grandmother, mother and others had not lied to me; it wasn't possible that so many people should lie to you; my father was on a trip. But I didn't want him to have gone to Karbala. Maybe I had heard it wrong. But then I asked myself, 'Where's he gone then?'

I didn't dare ask grandmother. I feared that she might say he'd gone to Karbala, or that he was dead, both of which had the same meaning to me.

Summer was over. I returned to my mother. She didn't have any other children. She wasn't just a mother or a beautiful being for me; she was a fairy and the forty-braid daughter of the King of Fables. I loved my mother more than anything else in this world. It was because of her that I hadn't paid any attention to the absence of my father. Although she was a little strict and at times she would become stern and bad-tempered, her glowing beauty made me proud in front of the other kids. No other kid had a mother as beautiful as mine.

At nights when we were alone she told me stories, and her

warm familiar tone made everything she told me seem real and concrete. Sometimes she made paper dolls for me, folded and then unfolded them, put them in a circle on a round tray, and slowly and rhythmically snapped her fingers on the back of the tray, and I laughed at the dancing paper dolls. Sometimes she put them in couples between the lamp and the wall and moved them with a string, and their shadow on the wall became my little cinema. She had named the paper dolls 'the plum gang'. The dolls of the plum gang were real and dear to me; I would cry if one of them was torn apart. I never went near them in the mornings; their disarrayed condition on the tray disturbed me. But at nights, in the light of the brass lamp, I believed in them: they were real.

When I came back from grandmother's house that autumn, there was a change in our home. My mother stayed with me less frequently. There were a lot more comings and goings; maternal and paternal aunts came and went. Sometimes I got up and listened to them. I couldn't understand why they were speaking of someone who wasn't there and whom I didn't know; it seemed that a guest was expected; they kept talking a lot about him. Then there came a time when my mother was livelier and in higher spirits and took more care of herself; she sewed dresses, and sometimes when she was alone she whispered a song. This song wasn't like the ones she used to sing before; in those days she sang lullabies for me so beautifully that even when I grew up I would ask her to sing lullabies for me. In the dark cold winter nights, under the warm *korsi* and white sheets, she used to sing:

Lala lala, pennyroyals
My kid's come home
Lala lala, sweetbriers
My kid's come like a fairy
Lala lala pistachio flowers
My kid's come like a bouquet

But now she varied the pitch of her voice, sang the lines tactfully and I felt that she wanted to believe in what she was singing. At such times her voice trembled with doubt when I approached her. However, I loved her singing; even at nights when she didn't sing lullabies and just sang for herself, a vague feeling brought tears to my eyes. I ducked my head under the quilt and held my breath; I didn't want her to know that I was crying and to stop singing.

It was in those days that I gradually became agitated with a premonition, like an animal before the earthquake. I didn't know why. I guessed that my mother must have seen me when I was pinching some jam from the jar, or when I was taking her loose change from under the carpet, or found the broken plate I had hidden away, and found out that I'd done it. I approached her cautiously, I didn't nag any more, I didn't insist on her telling stories at night. I vowed to myself to become a good kid. One day at the time of the sundown prayers I vowed that if father came back from his trip or if mother became like she was before, I would not only abstain from blowing out the candles of the *saqqakhaneh*[1] opposite our house or making dolls from their leftover wax, but would also light candles on Thursday nights and give all my pocket money to that orphan kid with the Aleppo boil. I pledged not to use the chain of the water bowls of *saqqakhaneh* as a swing any more; I pledged to pick up bread crumbs from the pavement, kiss them and put them beside the wall so that noone would step on them. I had even decided to learn praying from grandmother.

One day our house became crowded. The rooms were cleaned and chairs were laid in them. In the corner room, a white spread was put on the floor; at the end of the spread was put the full-size mirror, which was a relic of my mother's first wedding and next to which used to be my father's portrait in the old days. Two bronze-

---

1.   Persian word for traditional public drinking fountains found on street corners. These votive fountains comprise a niche with a water tank, metal bowl and other items and usually contain the portrait of an imam, metal trays with candle-holders and small locks or pieces of rag fastened to symbolize pious wishes.

base lamps that had blue crystal bellies with gem-decked peacock motifs were lit. I was made to put on my velvet puff-breast dress and told not to wriggle around.

I went to the corner room across the yard. My father's portrait, which used to hang on the wall in the dining room, was put on the mantle in the corner room. My mother was also there, plucking her eyebrows with bone-handle tweezers. A swollen red crescent was imprinted above her golden glistening eye. I stood before her; I wished to talk to her but I couldn't. My father's portrait on the mantle had a fixed sad gaze. Maybe it was the first day that I was properly looking at my father's picture and imagined that he was looking at me. I wished that my mother would say something about him, but she was silent. She was wearing a *jujube* red tricot dress and her fair curly hair cascaded on her shoulders. She was pursing her lips like the times she sulked with me, and there was a tiny dimple under her chin.

She took a fleeting glimpse at me; for a moment all the trust I had in her came back to me. Now I was light-hearted and moved around the room playfully. When mother finished her job, I followed her to the dining room. But I let go of her at the cellar entrance. I had thought of calling on grandmother. I went down the stairs and found her standing at the oven, her face glistening with tiny droplets of sweat. She wiped her eyes with the corner of her headscarf and said, 'Don't come here, sweetheart, there's too much smoke, you'll hurt your eyes.'

Then she bent down and picked two of the small meatballs she had fried for making *fesenjan*[1] and handed them to me; for a moment she looked at me as I was eating the meatballs, then she hugged me and pressed my head against her chest. I smelled the smell of her body that was so familiar and dear; her headscarf smelled of smoke; I couldn't look at her face. With a voice that was on the verge of breaking, I said, 'Grandma, my dad's due to come tonight, right?'

---

1. Stew made from lamb meatballs in a thick sauce of ground walnuts and pomegranate paste.

And I held my head right there. Her heartbeat thumped against my cheek; I was waiting all over and I regretted having asked that question. How I wished that she would answer as late as possible, and the excitement that she would say, 'Yes, he'll come,' was clawing at my heart. I planned a thousand plans in a moment, but grandmother didn't say a word. I was afraid to lift my head and look at her, but she seemed to be trembling. I could hear her rapid panting; she pressed me to her breast; warm drops trickled onto my face. By now time was stretching too much. It seemed like the night had befallen and the guests had left. I lifted my head from her chest. She held my face in her hands, looked at me for a moment and wiped my eyes with her rough fingers. The wrinkles of her face had become more pronounced, but her resemblance to my mother remained even in those furrows. She said quietly, 'There's too much smoke here; go up, go, sweetheart; go get cookies from your uncle.'

I had bent over. I pressed my face against her cheek. It was moist and shivering. Through her headscarf, the red glow of the flames and the shadows they cast on the smoke-covered walls of the room made me think of hell. I asked, 'Grandma, you're crying?'

A deep sigh broke in her chest; she moved but didn't answer. I thought that despite all the vows I had made, I was still a nosy kid. I left grandmother and climbed the stairs without saying a word; midway I turned and looked at grandmother: she was rotating the skimmer in the big pot and stars were quivering on her face and suddenly her face assumed a crystalline redness from the log she put under the pot, and then was faded in smoke and darkness.

I ran to the dining room. It was full of men and women relations. Then a long-bearded man came who was wearing a fine black *aba*[1] and a muslin turban, and accompanying him was a goatee-bearded dwarf carrying a big book under his arm, the book disproportionate to his height. Both went towards the corner room. My mother was sitting there in front of the full-size mirror, her face glowing in the light of the lamps.

---

1.   A long thin robe that Shiite clerics wear over their cloak.

She took a look at me from the corner of her eye; I was about to jump into her arms but she bit her lip and I was electrocuted where I was standing.

There was disbelief in her gaze and I was stunned by her beauty. I missed her. After those days of parting, I wanted to speak to her; I had a hundred things to tell her; the smoke of *esfand*[1] and the terrifying voice of the bearded man and the silence that had fallen everywhere stopped me. At this moment my mother looked at me again, and the feeling in her look was different from the usual. I wanted to go kiss her, to hug her and to tell her all that was in my heart, tell her of all the vows and pledges, but then my mother dropped her head again, looked at the Koran and said something under her breath. The sound of clapping and joyful cheers broke out; I was scared and didn't notice who hugged me from behind and gave me a big rice cake.

It was almost two weeks after my mother's wedding; I was gradually realising that there was someone else in our house too. My mother's behaviour had improved. She gave me jam and loose change herself. At nights she told me stories of her own accord and we slept together. I used to press my head against her chest, put my hand on her breast and go to sleep. The smell of her body was so familiar to me that I could only go to sleep in her arms. Maybe I was a timid child, but my mother had never left me alone at night; it was different when I stayed with grandmother, but mother was something else; with her I wasn't scared of anything.

That night I dreamt that a black hairy hand came towards me as I was squatting, and drove me towards a pit. The pit was like a furnace; then I saw that it looked like the furnace of the *taftoon*[2] bakery down our alley; other kids and I used to throw pebbles into that furnace. In the world of my dream I suddenly thought of bad people on Doomsday: a blazing pickaxe was in the hairy hand; it wanted to hit me in the head; no matter how I tried I couldn't

---

1. A heavy incense of wild rue usually put on charcoal to protect one from the evil eye – as legend has it.
2. One of several kinds of flat breads traditionally baked in Iran.

shout; it was impossible; I was helplessly being dragged towards the pit of fire. My arms and legs were numb and inert and not under my control. Suddenly I saw my mother who seemed to be standing on the other side of the furnace; she was wearing the same *jujube* red tricot dress; she turned her face to me and bit her lip. I reached out my hand towards her; I was so glad to see her that I forgot my fear. I grabbed the hem of her dress; the dress was stretching in my hand and she was getting away from me. I let out a muffled shout and woke up with a jolt.

For a moment I didn't know where I was. I could still feel the heat of the flames on my cheeks. My body was shaking and my heart was beating so fast it was as though it wanted to jump out of my throat. I was gradually realising that I had had a dream, but I still didn't have the strength to move. I thought of my mother; I turned to hug her but she wasn't by my side. I felt that I was in a new bed. I slowly stuck out my head from under the quilt: across the room my mother and that man were asleep. They were covered by the flowered satin quilt that belonged to my mother's first wedding, the one I liked so much. My mother's head was resting on that man's arm and her flowing fair hair was spread on the pillow and the moonlight had cast a blue glow on some of its locks.

In summer I was sent to grandmother again. Although I didn't do anything bad, I realised that I was losing my mother. She was as kind to me as in the past, but I felt that I didn't have the right to be with her like I was in the past. Her body was bulging out, she walked awkwardly and she didn't sing any more. When she sometimes told stories she was not as patient as before. She shortened the story and wrapped it up somehow; I didn't look at her and pretended to be asleep.

I was delighted when they sent me to grandmother. In her home I could find the same games and playmates. Best of all, I could be like I was in the past, as if nothing had happened. My only concern was my spoilt and naughty cousin. It was to escape from him that I played on my own. I made a garden, built a water canal, made a hedge with broom twigs around my garden and planted herbs in it. Best of all was watching the garden. Again the wild tulips and chamomile had blossomed and the mulberry tree of the snake barn had spread its umbrella, and this time round under the *jujube* tree, a curly black lamb was tied instead of the ginger goat kid, and it was baaing constantly. The only bad thing about these days were the long afternoons because I couldn't go to sleep. I wanted to swim in the pool but grandmother wouldn't let me. As she put it herself, she made fun of me, told stories for me, said whatever she could think of to put me to sleep. Slowly she got tired and fell asleep. The buzzing of the houseflies and the white shadow of the azure-washed curtains made me restless. A long, printed cloth curtain hung before the storage room; on it was a picture of Shirin swimming while Khosrow, on his horse, was watching her in awe and biting his finger. Behind them was the picture of blue sugar-cone shaped mountains on which Farhad was standing with a pick in his hand, and at the bottom of the curtain were lines of poetry.[1] I made faces at them; I tied the corner of grandmother's headscarf and tied in it the fortune of the fairy princess so that she would go wandering and grandmother wouldn't know. I played with the money pouch hanging from grandmother's neck. I liked its jangling sound. Then I became fed up. I made faces at the sleeping grandmother. I pulled my face and mocked her snoring. I wriggled

---

1. Khosrow and Shirin is one of the most famous love stories of Persian literature, composed by the poet Nezami (1140–1203 AD). Khosrow Parviz who lived 590–628 AD is said to have married a daughter of the Greek Emperor Maurice, named Irene, called by the Persians Shirin, or Sweet. Farhad's history forms a tragic episode in this romance. He was a sculptor, celebrated throughout the East for his great genius, and was daring enough to fix his affections on the beloved of the King. The jealousy of Khosrow was excited, and he lamented to his courtiers the existence of a passion which was so violent as not to be concealed, and which gave him great uneasiness. He summoned Farhad to his presence, and commissioned him to execute a work, which should render his name immortal – to clear away all impediments, which obstructed the passage of the great mountain of Bistoun. He commanded him, after having done this, to cause the rivers on the opposite side of the mountain to join.

so much that she woke up and put her arm round my neck and, as she would say, she put me down.

On that day I was wriggling just like that under grandmother's arm when the door opened with a thud and my uncle came back from work. Grandmother's sleep was deep now. Still, I would tell her that I was going to my uncle's room if she woke up. I pushed her arm off my neck, got up and ran away. I stood at the threshold of my uncle's room. From a packet he was holding, he took out a big apricot and gave it to me and then stroked my head. At that moment his naughty kid ran to him, pushed me back and hung on his father's neck. My uncle hugged him and lifted him up and looked at him for a while. The kid's face was dirty and his gaze was sheepish and meaningless. My uncle kissed him several times and then put him on his shoulder and went round the room and said:

'How I missed you, sweetie … from the morning … you were asleep when I left, how I…'

Gradually his voice grew distant. The sour flavour of the apricot assumed an acrid taste in my mouth; I ran to the courtyard and spat in the pool's drain and I don't know what happened that I went into the garden. At that time of day usually there was noone in the garden. I don't know why I went under the mulberry tree and sat there on the rotten leaves and started beating the soil with a dried weed.

The sound of beetles and crickets had surrounded me with a sharp, uninterrupted chain. The pungent smell of rotten leaves and ripe mulberries intermingled with the scent of dill and chamomile and parsley and made the hot afternoon air heavier. I felt like I was sleepy; my arms and legs had gone numb and the surrounding view was blurred and unfamiliar to me. Under the sunlight, fresh grass and flowers were trembling and rising to get closer to the sun. Suddenly all that I had seen hundreds of times before seemed new to me. The blurred dome and minaret and the thatched roof of our house had moved leagues away. I wasn't interested in anything. I felt like I was plunging into a strait. My body was one-dimensional and made of paper, like the dolls of the plum gang. I wished there were cool air. But I couldn't find that air. Something had settled on my chest.

I lifted my head from my knee and quit scratching on the rotten leaves. And it was only then that I realised the snake barn was in front of me. I had never come so close to it. I stared at its glassless windows. There, beyond the empty framework of the window, there was something: two oblique red snake's eyes were glowing. Its gaze was glazed and fixed. We looked at each other for some time. I wasn't scared of it, nor was it unfamiliar to me. For a moment I closed my eyes and plunged into the darkness inside me; there was nothing. There was nothing.

When I opened my eyes the snake was still looking at me, and in its eyes was the sorrow of exile.

Darkness had begun.

SHAHRNOOSH PARSIPOUR

Crystal Pendants

And on that day it struck me that these were crystal pendants. You see? There's absolutely no similarity between them. I don't know why I had thought that they were crystal pendants. I had gone round the corner when I saw their shadows on the wall, the shadows of tens of clusters that had been cast on the wall.

Before that was the memorial of grandmother. All the time when the Koran reader was reciting, my mother was crying and I was looking at the huge heap of wet mud that covered the outside of the tomb. A fine mild rain had been falling constantly since a few hours ago, and now the smell of moist earth and the scent of red roses my father had bought for grandmother's grave intersected at the landing before the tomb, and when the smell of the bodies of dirty mourning women sitting round the tomb penetrated it, you looked at a cloud outside the tomb inadvertently and you wished you could run away. That was why when it was over and mother dropped herself onto the grave and screamed and the howl of everyone suddenly soared, I had already stood up. The Koran reader was standing under the taffeta of the tomb's entrance and when I was passing him, I saw that he was looking at something between me and the wall, and his left hand was resting on the wall, and in his right hand he was holding the Koran; I had seen the waiting look in his eyes.

Out there, I could see that something was walking faster, much faster than me, and I had to keep walking on the graves rapidly with mud-covered shoes and the *chador* sticking to my legs, and the rain that was still falling constantly and in fine drops, had made my *chador* wet and was gradually permeating to my hair and the bare skin of my arms. By the time I reached the cemetery gate, I was fed up with the muddy and heavy *chador*. It was then that I took the *chador* off and ran my paws through my hair that had become disheveled and painful from the constant pressure of the *chador*, and I drew in a deep breath that was in its entirety the perfume of the rain, and I looked at the crude rain-soaked gravestones that had a bluish hue and were glistening; and suddenly it struck me that they were crystal pendants. The first time I came here – a year ago, more or less, I don't know – anyway, the first time I came here, the clusters were something in the order of an illusion, in the order of an irrelevant dream. I had not seen the crystal pendants then. Maybe it was winter, maybe it was sunset, and there was no longer any sun to cast any shadow. And the point is that, whatever it was, it was by this very wall. Hours before that, there was a situation that made me flee home. When I went round the corner, I saw him standing by this very wall. Perhaps I knew beforehand that he had been standing there. Perhaps that was why I had a familiar, embarrassed look on my face. Like a girl going to her first date. He was standing there, daring and tall. His long legs were wrapped in green velvet pants, showing all the twists of his firm muscles. His body was strong, like young, twenty-three year old elm trees; and the clothes could not contain all those young muscles; evidently it seemed as though he should get undressed on the beach and invite his body to the feast of water and the sun. The alley was too narrow for him.

When we came face to face, I could see that his eyes were burning me; that they went through my entire being. And this was a bad sign that had disturbed my entire soul; that had agitated my thoughts. It was then that I noticed that his tone bore no resemblance to those daring eyes. First he had said, 'Well, let's go.' And he had said this in such a manner that some of my self-confidence returned, and I took a fresh breath. But my breath was still choking in my throat, and this silence had made him think that this was a kind of fight. Besides, there was also the darkness, and the dim light of the lamp at the end of the alley had only lit his face, and I was in the dark, and perhaps this bothered him who was waiting for my answer, and in the feeble light, I was rolling my eyes to find a way to escape, and I saw the shadow of the plane trees and the disturbed dream of the clusters; and I noticed that he had no shadow, and that he himself was an ambiguous outline of a shadow. Once again I heard him speak, 'Your eyes glitter.' He said this in such a manner that I thought he pitied me, and I was so numb with his being without a shadow that inadvertently I squatted on my toes. And he had sat with me, and this scared me. In order not to let him see my fear, I said, 'I wish I were two!' and he, sitting with me, had said, 'I wish I were two!' Perhaps he was also scared of me. I was constantly looking for something to say, looking for a word to break our painful silence with. I would like to speak of my grandmother's sugar-pot, which was silver and was embossed in black. I would like to speak of my brother's leather tobacco pouch and of the path, which was narrow and could only let one person pass at a time. When I go the whole way I'll get to a bus station.

I had said these things. He said, 'Well, that's why I say let's go. Why the bus? We'll go back from the direction you came. Once we go down the bend, the path will be open.' I was trying not to listen to what he was saying. I intended to keep him busy and pass by him in a flash when he was distracted. I was wondering if I could hit him hard against the wall and go past him. In my brain I had put my thoughts in order; but he was sitting right in the middle of the alley and his hands were touching the wall on the two sides. There wasn't even a little room to pass, and he was sitting very resolutely, just like when you're making plans to quickly go past someone else. Then the night had become blacker, and its dark dirtiness contaminated me, and I felt an urge to immerse myself in water; stand under some running water that would wash away, wash away, wash away.

'What's the use?'

This I had said, and he had replied, 'We can go just straight on until we get to the wide stretch.' I could only see the lights of the bus station at the end of the alley. I knew that you could sit there on metal benches and get the fatigue out of you, and while the fluorescent lamps were pouring light, you could feel their light on your skin, and if the bus was delayed you could read a newspaper and think about the news of the day.

Then a time had come when both of us knew it. He said, 'You pass first.' I didn't agree and he had sensed it. That was why he came towards me without a word. I pressed myself against the wall; now the shadow was behind me and my heart pounded like a headless chicken, and our bodies were about to become one for a long moment; and our glances were intertwined. At the bottom of his eyes there was something that you could say was a state between crying and a feeling like regret.

I remember that for a few moments I had thought like mad, and his coming round the curve of the last narrow alley; and only a sound of sobbing could be heard. Was he crying?

Then I ran down the alley quickly and got to the bus station. The station was drenched in light. Hurriedly I sat down beside a young man who had a newspaper in his hands, reading it carefully, and I noticed that all the waiting passengers were looking at me in astonishment. I wished to hide myself in the light; I wished to shrink, shrink so much that nothing of me could be seen any more. I was squirming where I sat, watching from the corner of my eye the people who were staring at me in shyness and perplexity. It was then that I noticed that I had no shadow, and that was why the shy, silent and kind people in the bus station were looking at me like that; the people whom I thought would welcome me easily among themselves, and we would set out together from the same station and in the same bus and go to a place where there was only light and grass. I was embarrassed; I was too ashamed to look into their eyes. Being without a shadow is a painful plight.

But were they really looking at me? I had time to think before the bus came. My whole body was boiling and sizzling from inside; but like when it's cold, there was also numbness, and besides all these things, I had been sitting in a manner that any passerby could suppose that I was quite comfortable. I was leaning my shoulders against the back of the bench and I had stretched my legs as far as I could, and the people were looking at me or at something else, and when I took a closer look I noticed that they were not looking at me, but at the things behind me. It seemed to me as if the people were taking pity on themselves, and that was why they had a kind look. It looks as if people always pity themselves when they are alone; and in the bus station everyone was alone in himself.

When I went down the bend, only our house was there. In the five-door room, grandmother was sitting as always. I mean, she wasn't sitting, for her shadow wasn't on the wall. I saw her only after I went in. She was snoring in her bed. Mother said, 'Bring torbat.'[1] I went out of the room. Looking from the outside, the shadows of mother and Dayeh Khanom were cast on the wall; their heads were elongated and when they turned into silhouettes, you could see the intangible movements of their lips. Maybe they were reciting the Prayer for Precarious Death. In my room, when I looked in the mirror, I was old, and two deep lines ran from my nostrils to the bottom of my chin. When mother came, she did not realise at all that I was older than her. She sat on my bed, and her hands were lying on her numb and shapeless knees. I had become

---

1. In Iranian tradition, the dying person is normally placed in a comfortable position facing Mecca. A few drops of a spiritually blessed water, called *ab-e-torbat* are put in the mouth to bless him or her. The water is supposed to be imported from Karbala, where Shiite third Imam Hussein is buried.

older. Mother said, 'It's a year that she's been in death agony; what reprise is she being punished for?' I didn't know. Mother said, 'It's the fifth time I'm pouring *torbat* water in her mouth. I'm ashamed of myself.'

During all that time when she had been in death agony – and it was months – I either walked under the trees or walked in my room. The room had a mirror and a chandelier and whenever I walked in the room, the colourful hues of the chandelier were on the opposite wall, and from there they were reflected in the mirror. That was how I saw the chandelier in the mirror, and my own shadow was never among the colours. I covered my mirror with a piece of black cloth. When I was outside, I could see that the leaves were blossoming again. Then there was a rain shower, and grandmother died with the first drops. We took her to the cemetery. The Koran reader was reciting, and I was in the corner of the tomb, and during the entire time that my back was against the wall, the rain was falling. There was no way for light to penetrate the tomb. Nobody's shadow could be seen there. That was why panic left me. When I went forward they had already covered the grave. Father told the Koran reader to say Horror Prayers till morning; and when my mother screamed the Koran reader was standing in the doorway. The uncut gravestones were drenched; they were piled up in a corner, and it was still a long way till sunset; that is, it was a very long way. Then I was here; perhaps it's for the sake of the clusters, whose colour is something between milk and honey. These are daisies. When light reaches them, it refracts and casts their shadows on the wall; on the contrary, the crystal pendants let light through easily and light becomes something among seven colours – so that they'll perfect illusion in you; so that you'll always be horrified.

BEHJAT MALEK-KIANI

O, Baba! O, Baba!

Zabol was asleep and the Hamoun was awake.[1] A tiny strip of water glittered at the bottom of the Hamoun, thick like congealed honey, with a heavy and inert margin.

I was standing by the Hamoun, watching it. How black and meandering it was. Half an hour ago when I woke up with a start, I found out that as always my man wasn't beside me. His bed was rumpled. I knew where he was. It was about a year that at midnight, when everyone was asleep, he left his bed. I knew that he was again sitting by the Hamoun now, talking to it. If I listened a little more intently I could even hear his voice talking to the Baba Mountain and cursing.

I came out of my bed; my kids were sleeping here and there in the room; they were breathing slowly. Sometimes one of them talked in his sleep and moved his arms and legs. I went out to the

---

1. Zabol is a city in Iran's southeastern Baluchestan province. Hamoun is a lake in the same region, where the River Hirmand, originating from Afghanistan, ends.

Hamoun to find my man. I knew he was there: he had nowhere else to go. I could hear his voice from far off. I sat down by the Hamoun and looked at it. I don't know why at that moment I imagined that the Hamoun was alive, had motion and feeling; as if it was thinking; perhaps it was thinking of raindrops and fresh streams of water; perhaps it was thinking of little ducks and bamboo. And it was fluttering like a fish out of water. Suddenly I felt pity for the little fish and ducks. Poor things didn't have fresh water and they were surely nauseated by the stinking oozing muck. I started walking again. I had to find my man and take him back home. His voice was coming from far off. He was cursing the Baba Mountain. I could hear him shouting:

'O, Baba! O, Baba! I'll take out your eyes with my very hands. I won't let you see the grief of my Hamoun; I won't let you pour the waters of thirsty lands into your dark. I'll rip your body apart with these very hands; I'll chew your stony heart with these very teeth; I'll drag your Hirmand out of your claws, I'll pull off her hair with my paws.'

I can hear the voice of my man crying out loud, and I can see his dried-up, narrow shadow on the sand: trembling and gathering his teardrops with its fingertips and dripping them into the Hamoun:

'Come, Hamoun, let these fresh teardrops be yours; maybe these teardrops of mine, these tiny drops, will fill your mouth. Why, you used to be our benefactor; you used to be so great for us; you used to be a mother to us; you used to be milk. How come all that milk dried up, the mother died ... and us kids withered away? You know, I'm saying this quietly to you: it's several days that my wife hasn't lit the baking oven to bake bread, my kids haven't got fresh bread in hand, the leather bag of milk is dried up, there's no oil left in the goatskin, there's no yoghurt on our spread. Ahoy, Hamoun! Poor little ducks have all died, little fish can't be found any more either. O, Hamoun! O, Hamoun!'

I hear his moaning getting louder every moment. I'm approaching him. I see him sitting by the Hamoun, drawing some things on the ground with his hand. At times he raises his head towards the sky, reaches out his hands towards the mountains and sighs again:

'O, Baba! You know, our cows have also died, our farmlands have been burnt. How could you have the heart to suck the juice of the clouds? To fill up your Hirmand and leave my Hamoun dry …? No, my Hamoun won't dry up. I'll fill it with water with these very hands, I'll bring back to life its little ducks and fish. I won't let my Hamoun flutter here before my eyes and dry up; I won't.'

I laid my hand on the bony back of my man and said, 'Get up man, get up and go to bed! You know that Baba doesn't hear our words; he has ears of stone. He'd have done something for us by now if he were able to hear us.'

He looked at me with his red, half-closed eyes, as if he didn't know me; as if he was looking at a stranger. I lifted him off the ground and took him home and put him to bed. But I was sitting there awake; I don't know why I couldn't sleep. I got up and went out. Before my eyes were clay houses and dried-up, cracked-up lands that until a few years ago were covered with wheat at this time of year, and we would sleep by these wheat fields at night. I don't know why I was reminded of the past, the time when Hamoun was full of water and its mouth wasn't parched and foaming like this. When night fell, its entire body gleamed and shivered. We used to launch our boats and wander around on the water. Sometimes men would catch fish. Happy memories! Good old days! Everywhere was green; in springtime narcissuses blossomed; I put a bunch of narcissuses in the water bowl and everywhere smelled of flowers. Our cows and sheep grazed well and had plenty of milk; I milked them in a bucket and extracted the oil. What beautiful yellow oil! I poured it into the goatskin and gave it to my man to take it away and sell it. There was always yoghurt and sour milk on our spread. In the morning when I finished sweeping the room and doing the housework I would go over to the oven and bake bread: what bread! Red and white, and I stuffed it with aniseed, the scent of which would fill everywhere. I baked bread mornings and evenings;

we always had fresh bread. My kids would gather round the oven, their little faces glowing with the fire from the oven, and they kept nibbling on bread, and what bread!

I was immersed in such thoughts when I got to the bank of the Hamoun; I sat and fastened my headgear. It was just last year when my man went insane. Before that he used to be cheerful. He went to the farm every day. Our wheat crop was very good; we also had a small garden with ruby grapes, and we had some chickens and roosters and cows and sheep in it too. We were well off; we didn't have a care in the world. But when the Hamoun dried up so did our lives. Wheat wouldn't grow and the garden had no water. The cows and sheep ate paper and grew thin. How my man used to grieve at that time. All the time he was thinking about Hamoun's drying up. And in the end, we had to sell our land and sell our cows and sheep. We wanted to leave Zabol and its Hamoun behind and go. But where to? We didn't know. Eventually we would find a place where we could find a loaf of bread to eat. I'll never forget the morning we were to sell our land and cows and sheep. I woke up in the early morning to make tea, but my man left without drinking tea to tend to the cattle. My man took the animals and left, and my kids and I followed him. We were supposed to sell them all to Meaty Esmail. He was waiting for us at the door of his house, as though he enjoyed dealing with us. Once he set eyes on us he started talking about how worthless the cows and the land were and he kept degrading us, haggling over their prices; in the end he bought such good cows and the land for less than half the price, and totted up the money and gave it to my man, who took the money and put it on the ground, next to his rumpled jacket. He was still speaking to Meaty Esmail, haggling with him; we were standing round them, looking at them with open mouths. I went inside Meaty Esmail's house to say goodbye to his wife. After all, we were supposed to set out and leave Zabol. When I came out of the house, I saw that there was a crowd at Meaty Esmail's door: my man was sitting on the ground, beating his head with his hands. When I stepped forward, I was told what had happened: the cows had eaten the greasy bank notes Meaty Esmail had given to my man. They were hungry and they had swallowed our whole life. Since that time my husband went insane and we stayed here; stayed by the Hamoun so that one day, maybe one day the Hamoun would be filled up again. Now every night, my husband comes to the Hamoun, and sits and talks to it. He curses and threatens the Baba Mountain.

I started towards home; in the darkness I could see my house; it looked as if it had been hit on the head; its roof was low and its walls were made of clay bricks. A little farther was Meaty Esmail's house. Its new door and windows glittered. In those days Meaty Esmail was doing very well because all the Zabolis were selling their cows and sheep to him and leaving town. And Meaty Esmail took the cows and sheep to towns here and there and sold them.

Meaty Esmail wasn't well off before the Hamoun dried up; he didn't even have a piece of land. His hands and clothes were always smeared with the blood of cows and sheep. But today his wife and kids walk in Zabol with their noses in the air, mocking us who once used to be landowners. Their *chadors* and shoes are new and clean, and their lamb stew is always boiling on the fire. Oh, my poor old man, how could you know what the world had in store for you? If you had known, you wouldn't have worked day and night like a horse on that farm and you wouldn't have ruined yourself for the sake of the cows and sheep. But what can be done? The world is like that: it's got ups and downs.

I wish it weren't midnight; then I could go to Nanneh Sorour's house, start up her hookah and get some nice smoke into me.

FERESHTEH MOLAVI

Midnight Drum

He's just left; he'll be back soon. He said himself he'd be back soon, very soon. Maybe in an hour; or at the most, if he forgets his word and his promise and his vow, he'll be back by ten. She's washed the dishes. She's put the kid to bed. She's again left undone the undone sewing job. She's again closed the half-read book. She's unwound the hobble of restlessness for another evening.

Maybe she'd better go to bed. For the last time, she calls on the kid and pulls up the blanket that has slipped down over her. She winds the alarm clock. Plugs in the electric insect repellant. Turns off the lights. Before going to bed, tired and sluggish, she hesitates. In her mind, she goes through nocturnal duties one by one and thoroughly. She's fulfilled them all – all the tiny and trivial household duties. A habit that has become an obsession, but still unaccomplished: she goes to the window and stands there; half-crouched, elbows on the dust-covered narrow sill, chin in hands. Is the blue dome high and far away, or low and close by? Is the moon hidden or visible? Are there clouds up there or stars?

Tonight there's a full moon; it keeps appearing and disappearing. It crawls without haste behind the hasty fragments of cloud, softly sliding on them; goes with the cool October breeze and breaks up on the dull water of the pool.

Her knees bend. Irritably she throws herself on the bed. She pulls the blanket over her head and closes her eyelids. Tonight, the night of relief from submission, she should be at peace. The nights he's at home, the nights she keeps wandering in the kitchen until he goes to sleep, the nights she pretends to be sick or weary, the nights she submits without passion or love, or the nights she surrenders to the raw and unrefined need of her own body – the nights smeared with deceit and hypocrisy or fear and submission – on such nights it's no wonder there's no trace of peace. The night of solitude shouldn't be devoid of peace, however. If this night had not been polluted with the poison of waiting, she would have found peace and tranquility from the nocturnal quiet. The day, with its staring brightness, its incessant movement, with a load of work and duty, conceals all fears and anxieties in itself. The night, however, with its darkness and stagnation, tears apart the deceitful veil of the day, leaving it exposed, unprotected and without shelter in a breathtaking current. Why won't sleep come to her – a sleep without dreams or nightmares? Why doesn't she become free of the temptation of escaping from an undisputable submission? Why doesn't she get up to take flight in the fancy of a fearless rebellion?

The sound of a car engine falls over the soundless moaning of her anguish. Inadvertently she pulls aside the blanket and sits motionless on the bed. She listens intently. What should she do if it's him? Sit and throw it in his face that she's been waiting for him and blame him in silence? Or grumble and get it off her chest? Or, best of all, pretend to be fast asleep? The sound approaches and goes away. It gets lost and leaves the alley and her to themselves in its excited silence.

She throws the thought of sleep out of her mind. She sits at the edge of the bed and stares beyond the window. A half-cloudy, half-moonlit patch of sky in the repulsive metal frame, a garden immersed in an anguished illusion, and a small pool with a little water in it – all her share from the expanse of the night outside. She can modestly say in her heart that it's not such a bad share after all. Her share of the inner night is greater, though.

She must get up; maybe she can shake this dust off her body and soul. Again she stands by the window. Again she stares at the half-bright and half-hidden moon – the same moon she used to stare at while waiting; a moon whose beauty and kindness neutralised the poison of waiting. No, this moon is not the same moon. She isn't young enough any more to be happy with an imaginary love and she is not old enough to rest in peace with a heart devoid of desire. It's the moon of October. A cold October. The house is silent. A cold silence. If her husband is running away from this creeping, precarious cold … No, he can't. It's not a matter of rights. None of them own any right, or love or affection. Both are chained to a deceitful, painful bond. They're not equal, though. Identical punishment for non-identical sins; or perhaps for unequal sins. Their remedies aren't the same either. Her husband pretends to be omnipotent. He goes wherever he wishes, says whatever he wishes, does whatever he wishes. Although made from deceit just like the man's remedy, hers has another colour and flavour. The man deceives himself more; in return, he is relieved more. Her inevitable cure is the old cure of female submission – a submission polluted with hypocrisy and meekness and cunning. A deceit that conceals her desperation, but makes her wound more painful.

Her knees become numb and slack again. She throws herself on the bed again. She listens to the deep sound of her daughter's breathing. She immerses her face into the pillow and presses her eyelids hard together. She had fallen asleep. She goes to sleep. There is a sound. The sound was getting nearer. She didn't want to be pulled out of her sleep. She rolled over. There was emptiness at her side. She told herself, 'He's gone for a stroll.' The sound pounded on the delicate surface of her thin sleep. They were riding on water.

It was sunset. The seawater was green – the greenest of greens, like a wheat field. The wheat field was the greenest of greens. They were standing in the middle of the wheat field. The bird was wheeling up there, in the middle of the azure dome. With the silken web of his song, the bird was sewing the patches of cloud together. Behind the curtain of the horizon, the sun was sinking into the sea. The boatman was staring at the horizon. Restless and in love, in the middle of the wheat field, she stood staring at him plough the soft and moist earth with a piece of wood. The bird was wheeling up there in vain. She bent over the edge of the boat and thrust her hand in water. She felt the warmth of her husband's thigh, but she was plunging into the joyful fantasy of making love to the water. The sharp, shrill sound of a bird tore the satin of her dream apart. With eagerness full of longing, the man stood staring at a young girl and boy who were sitting close to each other at the other end of the boat. She was furious. She wanted to prod him, but she changed her mind. She looked away. Again she thrust her hand into the soft, dry earth. Again she closed her eyelids.

The sound was pounding more powerfully every moment at the peaceful curtain of the dream of a woman who is relieved of the breathtaking upheavals of a hackneyed love without any feelings of regret. The sound came forward; behind closed eyelids, it came forward through the narrow, uneven cobblestone alleys of Istanbul, dropping on her travel-weary body. She pressed her face deeper into the pillow. She didn't want to know which sound was so ruthlessly swallowing the quiet melody of her daughter's breath. The sound kept pounding, tearing to pieces the delicate warp and woof of her dream. She had got up in fury and sat in bed. Her husband was standing by the window, smoking a cigarette. He hadn't gone anywhere. Wounded by her indifference and frigidity, he was leaning against the corner of the wall, looking out into the alley through the lace curtain. She had asked, 'What's this sound?' Without looking at her, he had said bitterly, 'It's the waking drum. The drum of Ramadan midnight.'

They were walking through alleys, crying out. The shadows were coming forward, crying out something. The drums woke all those who were still sleeping. Sleep had left her eyes. She had woken up and seen that she was no more in love. It was as if the drums were crying out her release from the old love. On the roofs and in the alleys they were beating the drums of the disgrace of a woman who was no longer in love with her husband, a woman who, sleeping next to her husband at night, dreamed of obscure and nameless strangers, and apprehended and shameful during the day, put on the mask of a chaste and obedient wife. It was as if the drums were tearing apart all the curtains of deceit from her body and soul.

The pounding 'tom-tom' of the midnight drums of those remote years and the cries of hidden scandals are still imprisoned behind her eardrums. In sleep or in the quiet of lonely nights, her head becomes giddy with the swift, maddening pounding of the drums. The shadows come forward and the drums cry out. She becomes naked and disgraced. She is anticipating the sound of footsteps or the ting of the doorbell. She is longing to hear some news. With a poison-clogged throat, she keeps waiting – a black waiting, contaminated with hatred and a longing for the man's death.

The horror of the onslaught of the scandalizing sound rocks her. She starts. Darkness, loneliness, shivering of the body and familiar sounds – the sound of a car's engine, the sound of footsteps, the sound of the turning of a key in the lock. Another night has come to midnight. Another night is ripped to shreds by the roaring 'tom-tom' of the drums. Another night the man comes back home to blind her sinister, anticipating eye with his presence.

MANSOUREH SHARIFZADEH

The Stranger

Yesterday was a very bad day. That is, it was bad for me. You know, yesterday was the first day of the New Year. But our house was in sorrow. When mom opened her suitcase to put her clothes in it, for a moment I felt that a huge grave had opened its mouth to swallow my entire being. I wished I could shout with all my soul and say, 'Mom, for God's sake don't go.'

But my throat being choked with tears, I could not utter a single word. Poor things Amir and Nader and Zohreh; how bitterly they cried. Zohreh has been incessantly crying since yesterday when mom left. She says, 'I've bought clothes to go to uncle's place with mom.' Amir and Nader have gone to the other uncle's place and now I've been left with this damned house; it's as if its walls and doors are choking me.

Mom is very discreet. I would have never imagined that someday mom would be forced to leave us behind and go. Particularly because she didn't spill anything in the past month so that we would not get bad marks in our second semester exams. Before leaving, she put her gold ring on the shelf and said under her breath, 'If Aqa Jan doesn't take it, you keep it.'

When my glance fell upon it, I felt as if a pot of boiling water had been poured over my head. The gold ring was shaking before my eyes; the gold ring that was mom's only ornament; Aqa Jan had put it on her finger on the very day of their wedding, and it had immediately fell out off mom's finger because it was too wide. It hadn't even fitted her middle finger. Mom said it had finally fitted her finger when she gave birth to Brother Mahmoud.

Since yesterday Zohreh has been continuously bragging about why mom didn't take us with her. I don't know what to say in reply. A couple of times I have tried to stall her, but she keeps pestering me. I want to tell her, even assuming that mom could take us with her, where was she supposed to take us? She's living in uncle's cellar, and after a lifetime of living with dignity, now she has to put up with the manners of uncle's wife. In those days when Aqa Jan was a labourer, mom used to do sewing, and uncle's wife was her apprentice. She was a nice girl and mom suggested that uncle marry her. And uncle liked the idea and accepted it. Now mom has to undergo ... But Zohreh can't understand such things. I said, 'Later when she buys a house, she'll take us there.'

Zohreh said immediately, 'But mom's got no money, absolutely no money. I looked into her purse. I saw it myself. Here it is.'

I looked with astonishment into mom's purse that Zohreh was holding. She was right; I had told a big lie; mom had no money at all. When she was leaving, she took a bus ticket from Amir and put a few toomans of loose change beside her ring and said, 'I came here one day with an empty purse; now I'm going back with an empty purse. It's God who provides for one.'

Mom was right. She was thirteen when they had married her to Aqa Jan. That is, she had just finished her sixth grade when Aqa Jan asked for her hand. They were neighbours and as Aqa Jan said, in those days he had fallen in love with her beautiful eyes. At first, they refused to agree with the marriage, for Aqa Jan was twenty years older than mom and also because Aqa Jan had no money. But Aqa Jan had threatened to kill mom and her future husband at any price if they didn't give her to him. And these threats had put a panic into the heart of grandfather, so much so that he had been forced to give mom to Aqa Jan. Mom said that while doing her hair the hairdresser had quietly asked her, 'Who found this husband for you?'

Tears had filled mom's eyes; she herself said so. Then the hairdresser had been startled and told her not to cry, otherwise her makeup would be ruined.

Later Aqa Jan's business flourished and after some time he entered a partnership with the factory's owner. Brother Mahmoud, who's abroad now, used to say in those days, 'Aqa Jan would never have made good if mom hadn't been around.'

And my grandmother – God bless her soul – used to say, 'My dear, don't put so much pressure on yourself; don't be obsessed with making this man rich. The guy that I know will be very difficult to harness once he's made a little dough.'

In those days I didn't understand the meaning of these words; but when mom left yesterday, it was as if all those words hit me in the head like a cannonball. I say, why did mom work so hard and keep still although she heard such remarks? What things I think of! Mom was the one who, even this last month that she had decided to leave, had told Aqa Jan for our sake, 'I can't stay in this house any more. Let the kids go through their exams this month, and then divorce me.'

What was mom's fault, honestly? She just worked and suffered all the time without uttering any complaints. She didn't even once asked Aqa Jan to buy her clothes or stuff like that. If someone brought a souvenir she would wear it; or if Aqa Jan brought some clothes for her from a trip she would put them on; otherwise I never saw her ask Aqa Jan for anything.

Amir said, 'Although mom's getting on a bit, she's still prettier than the stranger.'

By the 'stranger' he meant Aqa Jan's wife. As if knowing that something might happen if he stayed home, Aqa Jan decided to go to uncle's house early in the morning. That is, they told me to take care of Zohreh's affairs and go with them, but I said that I had a headache and I would stay home. To be honest, it's impossible for me to see uncle's wife with that smiling face – definitely smiling, because she always envied mom. When leaving, Aqa Jan frowned and said, 'We have guests for dinner; you know how to cook, don't you?'

It was the first time Aqa Jan talked to me like that. I knew that by 'guest' he meant his new wife. A few nights ago, there was a party in uncle's house. Aqa Jan had brought his wife along. That is, ostensibly as his friend's wife; and he introduced the woman's brother as her husband. But uncle's wife told us that she was Aqa Jan's wife. Mom wasn't there. She had stayed home to look after Zohreh, who had fever. Uncle's wife said that he'd wanted her to see us indirectly. There was a cunning smile at the corner of her lips when she said this. I felt something weighing heavy on my heart while uncle's wife was speaking. Aqa Jan's wife was sitting at the other end of the room and she had crossed her white legs. She had painted her toenails red. Amir looked at her furiously and she immediately pushed her skirt over her legs. I wanted to tell Aqa Jan that if mom went out into the street like that, she would definitely still be a 'darling' to you. Then I remembered that mom said that when she was young, Aqa Jan would castigate her when she went out without sunglasses; now it's not clear how the same Aqa Jan has put this one on display so generously.

When mom left, Amir said, 'Mom's flaw was that she was too chaste; when you grow up and marry a man, be careful not to become like mom; look what this stranger does and learn.'

I was too shy to tell him in response that as brother Mahmoud used to say ...

Apparently Amir had found out from my look what I was going to say, because he immediately said, 'I was just kidding; the dignity of a lady is above such things.'

He continued, 'You know Maryam, you're just mom's replica;

this gives me heart; otherwise, with what's happened I couldn't have stayed here even another moment.'

It's about one in the afternoon. My head is reeling and my hands are trembling. I went into the kitchen a couple of times and as soon as I set about cooking, I felt dizzy. I felt I couldn't work in that state; I took some bread and cheese and went into the room. I don't know why Zohreh had fallen asleep; no matter how many times I called her to wake up and have lunch, she didn't. Once she opened her eyes and said, 'Mommy ... my sweet mommy, you've come back to us; yes, you've come back to us.' And she closed her eyelids again.

Now I'm not in the mood to eat anything either; I'll keep sitting by Zohreh until they come back. They must come back in a couple of hours. I have made up my mind. Late afternoon we'll go together with the kids to mom and I'll tell her that we can't stay in this damned house, no problem, I know sewing, I'll work with mom. And at nights I'll study my lessons. But then the kids and I can be near mom. Now that Aqa Jan's become so estranged to us, the best thing to do is to leave. I'm sure that Amir and Nader will also agree. And Zohreh has no other wishes. We'll all go together and live in that very small house of uncle's. I'm sure that beside mom, the tiny cellar of that house can be as large as the whole world for us.

MONIRU RAVANIPOUR

The Blue Ones

1

Again the wind is howling. 'Hooo ... hooo ...' Swirling in the date palms, it brings everything with it and throws it all at the doors; the doors of the five-door room flutter. The boom of the sea is deafening, as if it wants to come in, reach out its blue hands and pick grandmother up and take her with it, take her where it keeps the fishermen. I put my arms round grandmother's neck, I kiss her – she smells of henna. Her hair and fingernails are henna-dyed. So are my hands. Today all the women of the village put henna on themselves. The men said it was over and the women put henna on themselves. Mansour's mother took henna from everyone, then she put it all into a huge cauldron that a hundred men had brought on to the beach and she made everyone put a bowl of sea water into the cauldron. My grandmother cheered; the women waved the wings of their net veils in the air, and Golpar and I danced. The men did the stick dance. Mansour poured a bowl of dry henna into the sea. The women cheered. A single bowl of henna is too little for the blue ones. Mansour's mother said, 'Pour it just for the sake of appearance. You know that even a thousand sacks of henna are too little for them.' Then the men of the village went to the sea. Several boats full of men … While pulling away from the shore, they waved their hands and chanted salutations to the Prophet and then they were so far away that their voices couldn't be heard any more and their boats had become the size of small bowls. We kept standing on the beach until they couldn't be seen any more; then I noticed that Golpar's mother was wiping her eyes. Bubuni was also crying. Mansour's mother said, 'Your eyes are always itching for a cry; go back to your homes now.'

Grandfather left too. He swore that she must have found him and that the sea was no longer to be feared. Grandmother didn't cry any more; she stayed like that on the beach and the women dyed her hair with henna; and when the cauldron was empty, she sat talking with Mansour's mother.

She said, 'Maybe they've detained him, maybe they've put chains on him.'

Picking the henna left at the bottom of the cauldron and putting it on her hair, Mansour's mother said, 'There's no use thinking, Madineh. We should have pity on ourselves. In two days' time the village will die of hunger; it doesn't matter who finds him, but we're doomed if they don't.'

It was three nights that her voice couldn't be heard any more. There was no wind and the sea was utterly still. Last night the men came to our house and sat with grandfather in consultation. Grandfather said, 'The sea wouldn't trick us, now would it? What do you mean it's quiet? Does it mean take up your nets and come on and that's it?'

Golpar's father said, 'Zayer Ahmad, one gets baffled; it doesn't mean that I'm scared; far from it … be it whatever you say, all right, we'll set out tomorrow.'

The men were confused. From behind the door I could see that their heads were down and some were playing with their toenails. In the end, my grandmother was furious. He waved his hands in the air and said, 'Whatever the matter, we shouldn't be paralysed, we shouldn't sit down to see what we shall do; who's going to answer the stomachs of your kids?'

After they left, the men were still indecisive and they were talking to themselves. Before going to sleep, grandfather kept saying, 'God forgive, God forgive.'

I slept with my grandmother; for three nights she slept peacefully and she told me stories about those who were blue and those who were red.

Tonight the wind is howling again. She surfaces on moonlit nights, when the moon is large, very large, as large as a round copper tray. If she comes again, my grandfather will never return. I'm scared; I cling to grandmother, who's not in the mood for me. When she comes, grandmother shouts at me and tells me that I've wrecked her nerves. On such nights she is bad-tempered and all her attention concentrates on the sea and she wants to hear all her words. Grandmother reaches out for the lantern, pushes the wick up and stands up and goes to her chest.

This morning Mansour's mother said, 'Madineh, if she comes again, we'll have to take the dolls out again. What's up? You mean she can't come and take them from the windowsills?'

Grandmother's chest is made of iron; when she opens its lid, its squeaking sound echoes in the room. Grandmother has rings, bracelets and brand new fabrics with which she wants to make colourful skirts, red, green and yellow skirts for when I grow up properly. She's got two iron dolls – one a man, the other a woman. The dolls are smaller than grandmother's thumb and Bubuni has so far borrowed them from her a hundred times to stick them together and put them under the fire, so that her husband would love her and would no more pocket the money he gets after he takes the fish to the town and sells them. Opening the chest's lid, grandmother sighs loudly and says, 'If only she could be wise enough!'

And then she talks to herself; she talks as she's searching in the chest. I stand up and go to her and sit by her and say, 'You're talking to me, grandmother?'

I know that she's not talking to me. In such times she forgets that I'm there and she talks to herself. 'Go to bed, kid!'

I don't move a muscle. Grandmother's hands are groping in the chest. The chest has a pleasant smell.

'She must have been ill; she's been ill these three days.'

'Grandmother!'

She looks at me recklessly. 'What is it now?'

'Maybe her grandfather and grandmother haven't let her come out.'

'Maybe.'

She resumes groping in the chest and brings the amulets out. She's tied them together: the heads of the dolls are coupled together. They're grey in colour. An iron man and an iron woman coupled together. Bubuni said, 'Thanks ever so much, Madineh; since I've put the dolls under the fire, he doesn't go to the harbour so frequently; thanks ever so much, Madineh.'

The iron dolls can only keep men at home, men who have wives like Bubuni who can't have children, and who keep making up their faces in front of the mirror all the time. Grandmother says that these dolls have no use for the kids, and therefore she wouldn't give them to me to put them under the fire, so as to overtake other kids when we go swimming in the sea.

Grandmother closes the chest, takes up the lantern and starts to go. I grab the hem of her skirt.

'Go to bed, kid!'

'I'm scared, I'm scared of being alone.'

I'm lying. I'm not scared of anything, not even of the Ghoul, which is bigger than grandfather, and Golpar and me wouldn't be more than a morsel for him. I want to see her again. She's so beautiful. She's blue and her face is blue too. Her hair is silver, like the colour of the sea. When it's early morning and the fishermen bring baskets full of fish to the shore, her eyes glitter every night. I'd like to go near her. Golpar says, 'Her dress is blue.' Grandmother says, 'Her flesh is blue.'

Grandmother opens the door: what a wind! The smell of henna has filled everywhere. The wind scatters the voice of Mansour's mother in the village.

'The amulets, women, the amulets!'

A large moon, very large, is sitting in the sky. When we reach the window that faces the sea, grandmother hangs the amulets and peeps through the bars. I can see her too: it's her all right; she's become a little thinner; she's come out of the sea and is sitting facing the moon. Moonlight glistens on the drops of water dripping from her hair. Her colour is blue. Grandmother says, 'The blue ones are kind.' Next morning we pick starfish with the kids. Every night that she comes, the beach becomes full of shellfish and starfish the following day. The voice of Mansour's mother has filled the village: 'The amulets, women, the amulets!'

The voice of Golpar's mother answers, 'We've set them up, we've set them up.'

Her voice trembles. She fears that the men will not return from the sea. The voices of all women who answer her are trembling. Grandmother is not thinking of grandfather. She's holding the window bars in her hands, and moonlight is cast on her face. Grandmother understands whatever she says. But I can only see her waving her hands at the moon. The wind scatters the voice of Mansour's mother in the village. She's yelling like sea captains, like when the sea becomes stormy and everything is in chaos: 'She hasn't found him … she hasn't found him.'

Grandmother replies, 'Go back to your houses; don't stand by the windows; she might get scared of us.'

We move back. The sound of her sobbing is like the sound of Golpar's sobbing. When her mother doesn't allow her to come for swimming she says, 'Hooo … m, hooo … m,' and then she shakes herself.

'Grandmother, when will she find him?'

She doesn't reply. When we're back in the room, she goes to the brazier, pushes away the ashes with the tongs, puts burning charcoal on the burnt tobacco and smokes.

'How thin she's become!'

'She's become so thin …'

It's useless. Grandmother isn't in the mood for anything. As long as her voice can be heard, she keeps smoking the hookah. I put my head on her leg, I take her hand and run it over my head, like when she's in a good mood and tells me stories and runs her hand over my head herself. The wind howls, she speaks and makes grandmother sorrowful. The wind comes in through the slits in the door. Just now the waves of the sea will destroy all the houses. Doors shake. It's as if someone is scratching the door with her blue fingernails. I'm scared. Someone is dragging herself along the ground. Grandmother drops the pipe of her hookah and goes to the door to listen. The sound is coming in through the window. I hide my face in grandmother's skirt. Evidently, she'll go for the amulets, gather all the amulets in the village and then take them with her and put them under the fire.

Grandmother says, 'Thank God.'

The sound moves away … it's rustling, as if stopping by all the windows. Grandmother and I come back and sit in bed. The voice of Mansour's mother rises: 'Hey, we're innocent, by God we're innocent.'

The voice of the women fills the village: 'We pray for you, we pray that you find him.'

'Keep our men safe, we've got kids to feed …'

'That's all the amulets we've got, we don't have any more.'

And the howling of the sea rises; she must have plunged into the sea. Sprinkles of the sea hit the door. Grandmother pulls down the lamp's wick. The sound of cheering fills the village.

'Now she'll be alright.'

'Go to sleep, kid!'

Grandmother's voice is cheerful and the wind takes the murmuring of the village's women to the bottom of the sea, where the blue ones dwell.

2

Everybody's gathered round the baking oven in the village square. Never before did all women come together to the oven. They would take turns to come. Now everyone's sitting around, some are baking bread and most of the women are sitting by the oven in the square, around grandmother and Mansour's mother. Grandmother says, 'No, not the blue ones … no …'

Golpar's mother nods. She's pale. 'What if something happens to them?'

Bubuni sighs, 'What beautiful hair she's got!'

Golpar and I are playing on the dirt near the women. We can hear their voices: 'Madineh, what the devil should we do if the men don't come back?'

'The blue ones don't drown anybody; it's the red ones that are nasty.'

'By God, if my Mansour doesn't return, I'll hold every blue one guilty …'

'Shhh, they'll hear and take it to heart.'

The men aren't back. Grandfather hasn't come back yet. Golpar says, 'Let's cry like she does.'

And she sits down, the way she was sitting last night, turns her head towards the sky and starts crying. I untie my hair and shake it loose round me and hold out my hands towards the sky. I start rocking and saying, 'Hoo … m … hoo … m …' Golpar's mother gets up from the oven, leaps and grabs her hair. Her voice is trembling.

'You wretched one, do you want her to curse us?'

Golpar breaks free from her mother's grip. She's truly crying. All the men of the village have gone. The blue ones are nice and kind, but if they curse, a thousand ships will sink. I fear that grandfather won't come back. I say a prayer and blow my breath towards the sea. They don't let us swim in the sea any more. Mansour's mother says, 'Noone set foot in the sea; anyone who does, there'll be no returning for her.'

When noon comes I go home. Grandmother comes back home from the oven and sits by the window. The window looks onto the village's main street. We can see anyone coming from the town. Bubuni said, 'With all these amulets we can bring back all the men.'

Grandmother says, 'Now that she's taken away the amulets, the fishermen must appear by sunset.'

'Grandmother, but there's no fire in the water!'

She turns and looks at me. Her eyes are the colour of palm dates.

'Their fire is different from ours … there must be fire, otherwise she wouldn't cry like this for a human being.'

'Grandmother, is that human being her grandfather?'

'No.'

'Then her father?'

'No, he's a fisherman.'

'She's crying so that he'll come and fish for her?'

'Yes.'

'Doesn't she know how to fish herself?'

'Yes, she does; she wants the fisherman to stay with her.'

'To swim with her?'

'No, to live with her.'

'Well, why doesn't she live with his grandma?'

'She lives with her too.'

'So what does she want the fisherman for?'

'She doesn't want to be alone.'

Now she must be putting the iron dolls under the sea fire. Green, golden, red and blue fish burn in the sea fire. Tomorrow the shore will be full of boiled fish. When the fish die, if the fisherman doesn't come back, she will be left alone with her grandmother and she will be sad.

Grandmother stands by the window till sunset. When the sun goes down she's tired. She looks at the sky and sighs. 'Tonight she'll drive the moon crazy.'

She wipes her eyes with the corner of her veil. The moon is far off. When night comes, I go and stand on the stairs. The moon comes, large, very large. Perhaps if I go to the rooftop I can catch it. It can't be done from the palm tree. I've tried that with Golpar. Grandmother doesn't allow me to go to the rooftop. Grandfather is tall and he can catch the moon.

'Grandmother, let's go to the rooftop and catch the moon!'

'Yes, let's give it to her so that he won't cry any more.'

'The moon is too far away, kid; besides, she doesn't want the moon.'

She answers me impatiently. I go sit by her side. I kiss her hair. Grandmother has a hundred braids. Her braids are long and henna-coloured.

'Why does she drive the moon crazy if she doesn't want it?'

'She wants the moon to show her a place.'

'What place?'

'The alley where the house of the fisherman was …'

'Doesn't she know herself?'

'No, she's lost the alley.'

'Do you know where it is?'

'Yes.'

'Then tell her.'

'It's useless; the fisherman has gone to a faraway place; and a mermaid can't get too far from the sea.'

'Grandmother, why did the fisherman leave?'

'Nobody knows. Maybe he was scared.'

'Of what?'

'I don't know. Gosh, don't ask so many questions!'

Grandmother is not in the mood to speak to me. Her braids sweep the ground as she is sitting. Like *her* hair that's so long that it sweeps the dirt when she comes out of the sea and sits on the dam facing the moon. The houses of the village can be seen through the window. No light comes out of any of them. If grandfather were here, the men of the village would come and sit and talk until late. My grandfather is tall. If he were here he would go to the rooftop and catch the moon. I count my grandmother's braids: one, two, three … there's too many of them. I say: 'Tonight she'll drive the moon crazy.'

She doesn't say anything. She's got a pair of green eyebrows that come together when I speak to her. Their ends reach each other. I play with her hair; she shakes her head, as if wanting to say, 'Leave me alone, kid!'

I ask, 'When will grandfather come back?'

'Noone will come back from the sea until the fisherman appears.'

The sound of the door of the yard can be heard. She's reached the stairs. She's talking to herself, 'Tonight is blacker than any other night; it scares the hell out of you.'

Bubuni comes in, puts her lantern in a corner. She always oils her hair and chews gum. 'Madineh, I was dying, I was so horrified.'

'Welcome … one can't stay alone these nights.'

'Yeah! I was afraid that the red ones would come and take me with them!'

'They don't take the women. They've got nothing to do with women.'

'But, Madineh, we've got tough luck.'

Bubuni sits down. Grandmother goes for the hookah. When she removes the hood, the wind howls. The booming of the sea rises suddenly. We all look at each other. Grandmother's voice is scared: 'Now she's going insane.'

Bubuni says, 'Our men won't come back any more … our men.'

The voice of Mansour's mother echoes in the village. Bubuni and grandmother go and shut the doors and windows.

'Shut them, shut the doors … don't look through the windows …'

She always used to come late, when the village was asleep.

Tonight she's come too early. Grandmother says, 'It's early evening. She's gone nuts.'

The sound resonates in the village: 'Hoo … m … hoo … m …'

Bubuni and I sit close to grandmother.

'Madineh, look how she moans …'

'Begging; she's begging. Let's go on the balcony.'

Bubuni doesn't come; she's scared and stays there in the room. It's moonlight. The moon is sitting above the date palms. When we reach behind the balcony window, I can see her. She's become so thin as if she's got tuberculosis. Grandmother covers her face as soon as she sees her; her shoulders are shaking. Grandmother loves the blue ones and curses the fisherman.

'May God make him go wandering for causing you such misery.'

And then, as if she wants the mermaid to hear her voice, she cries aloud and shouts, 'God have mercy on you, God have mercy on you.'

The moon is large and sitting in the sky; a piece of cloud approaches the moon, eats its edge, and slowly its claw covers the moon's entire face. She's waving her hands as if she doesn't know what to do any more. When the moon goes behind the cloud, she shakes and dives headfirst into the sea. I can see how she dives; she dives even better than Golpar. The waves of the sea hit our faces. We are wet. Grandmother hugs me. When we get into the room, Bubuni has shrunken in a corner and is trembling.

'Gone, Madineh? Is she gone?'

'Yeah! She's gone.'

'Our men, Madineh, our men!'

3

Mansour's mother said, 'The drums, the drums.'

'She won't come back any more; she'll just die there; she'd become so thin …'

Golpar's mother has taken her black clothes out of the chest; she still doesn't know whether to put them on or not. Golpar's cried so much she's become lean. Mansour's mother said, 'Beat them so hard that their sound goes to the farthest point of the sea. Either our men come back or their bodies will come to the shore.'

While drumming, Bubuni said, 'Harder, women; beat harder; maybe they've lost their way.'

Now it's three days we've been drumming. We sit by the shore and beat them; the women take turns to drum; everyone's hands are aching and it's three nights the moon hasn't come out; and she's nowhere to be seen either. Grandmother says, 'She's driven the moon crazy ... driven him crazy.'

Bubuni says, 'The moon knows what she's done to our men.'

Grandmother says, 'The blue ones are kind, but if they curse someone ...'

Grandmother's sitting, smoking the hookah. I gather her braids together. She says, 'Don't do it, kid!'

'Grandmother, why did the moon go?'

'Because he would have gone to pieces with sorrow if he'd stayed.'

If the moon goes to pieces I'll collect its pieces. Then I'll sit on the dirt and play with Golpar. Golpar's a poor darling; if the moon goes to pieces, I'd give most of the pieces to Golpar, so that when I go to visit her, she'll bring things for me in those pieces; besides, may be I'll give some pieces of the moon to grandmother to make a doll's face for her. Golpar loves to have a doll with the face of a mermaid.

'Grandmother, if the moon goes to pieces, will his pieces drop in the sea or on the palms?'

'The moon won't go to pieces; don't talk blasphemy; go to bed.'

'But you said he'd go to pieces.'

'I said he'd die of sorrow; human beings die of sorrow too.'

The night is black. Utterly black. The stars are lost. I put my arms round grandmother's neck. My grandmother has become thin and I'm afraid that she'll die of sorrow.

'Where's grandfather now?'

'God knows.'

'Is he fishing?'

'No, any kind of fishing would have been over by now.'

'Where is he then?'

She doesn't reply; she doesn't say where he is; but I know: If the mermaid curses someone, all will go to the bottom of the sea, where it's full of corals and starfish; they'll stay right there in the water, sit in the mermaids' houses and be sad. When she was in a good mood, grandmother said, 'You see sometimes the water in the sea comes up? That's when all the fishermen at the bottom of the sea start crying, when they miss their homes.' Now grandfather is crying too. He is missing the village. I wish the moon went to pieces! I wish the mermaid died … Where's my grandfather? … Grandmother says, 'Go to sleep, kid. Shut your eyes tight and go to sleep …' I close my eyes. Grandmother is awake, I know.

4

It's been a long time since the moon has stopped coming out; it's sunken there under a black cloud in the sky and sometimes it turns red. Like Golpar who turns red when she cries. Golpar's mother is dressed in black. Yesterday the women were dressed in black. They have put black flags above the doors. Bubuni didn't put a flag and said, 'He may come back.' Mansour's mother, who's very fat and had never cried, was walking ahead of everybody else in the village; black flags were on her shoulder, and when she reached a door, she set up the black flag and cried aloud and spoke of her Mansour. Mansour's mother said, 'My tall, handsome, young one, my unmarried young one, ah.' Then we all moved again and set up the next flag.

Bubuni said, 'No, they may come back; he may come back.'

Until sunset we walked in the village and set up flags. Grandmother is tired. She's very tired. She's stretched her legs; she's rubbing them with her hands.

'But you said the blue ones are nice.'

'Perhaps she has relatives too; she must have cursed.'

We go to bed very early. There is no light in any house. The flags flutter in the wind. When we lie down, someone knocks on the door. Grandmother says, 'Oh, Bubuni doesn't give up even so late at night!'

I say, 'Maybe it's grandfather.' Grandmother takes the lantern and goes. When she opens the door, I see her: she's blue and she's thin as a stick. Grandmother tells me, 'You don't come out.' And she goes. She goes with her, who's come stealthily and without forewarning. I'm scared. I'm scared that she may take my grandmother with her. She speaks, and grandmother says, 'No, you can't. By God you can't. You'll die. You did wrong. Why did you run away? Now they'll kill all the fishermen.' I'm scared that the sea may collapse on the houses. If the mermaids heave at the sea, we'll all sink underwater, and we'll become food for fish right there ...' She's still begging. Her voice is trembling.

Grandmother answers her with a sobbing voice, 'No, no, that's what you think. You'll die of sorrow; you'll become worse than now; see what you've done to yourself. You think you'll be relieved if you replace your heart with a human heart? The poor human heart is filled with sorrow. Okay, okay, I'll change it for you. But I'm telling you: you can't go far, it won't last even an hour.'

Her voice dies. What are they doing? Will she take grandmother with her? Will grandmother give her own heart to her and she won't recognize me when she comes back? I can hear footsteps, footsteps that are running ... it seems it's my grandmother running. Where's she going? Where's she taking her? Something drags itself behind the door, knocks on the door. It's my grandmother's voice that says, 'Open the door.' I jump up and open the door.

'Oh, grandmother! Where's she? Where's she ...?'

'Come give a hand. I gave it to her; she went off to find him …
Come, help.'

I drag grandmother onto the straw mat, a grandmother who's
half-fish. I pull up the lamp's wick. I sit away from grandmother and
look at the half of her that's blue.

'It's me all right kid, don't be scared; I just exchanged my legs.'

'Why, why did you go and become a grandmother for the fish?'

'She was dying; she would have died right here if I hadn't given
them to her.'

Grandmother's blue half glitters; I wish morning would come; I
wish Bubuni would come to our house again.

'Grandmother, when will she bring back your legs?'

'If she survives, soon.'

I'm scared; I'm scared of grandmother. I open the window and
sit by the window.

'Don't be scared. It's me.'

'I know, I know.'

I wish she would come back soon. What if my grandmother
jumps into the sea? I wish Bubuni would come. 'Grandmother,
shall I go and call Bubuni …'

Grandmother is not paying any attention to me. She's looking at
the window. She looks at the sky; her lips are trembling. The moon
slowly comes out from behind the clouds.

'Grandmother, the moon, the moon…'

She's crying. 'She's already dead! Already; I told her she
wouldn't …'

Grandmother is a fish; half of her is a fish. The moon has come out
and there's no longer anyone to drive him crazy. The mermaid has died
somewhere on the land. When she was in a good mood grandmother
used to say, 'Mermaids can't get far away from the sea …'

Now I'm sitting before her, half of whom is human. Grandfather
won't come back. He'll sit right there among the corals and be sad.
And I'm scared that grandmother will jump into the sea and go and
become a grandmother for the fish.

SHAHRNOOSH PARSIPOUR

Mahdokht

Mahdokht had planted herself by the river, in autumn, and she was moaning all through that autumn. Her feet were little by little freezing in the mud. The cold autumn rains tore up all her clothes. She was left naked with pieces of rag. First she was trembling until winter began. In winter she froze entirely. Her eyes had remained open, looking at the water all the time. The water was flowing.

Spring, with the first shower, broke the ice in her body. She realized that little buds were growing from her toes. The feet were growing roots. All spring she was listening to the sound of the roots growing. The root took the strength of the earth and sent it through her body. Nights and days, she kept listening to the sound of the roots growing.

In summer she saw the water turn green.

In autumn the cold came. She was not moaning any more. The roots stopped moving. The growth stopped.

In winter she fed on dewdrops. She was frozen but she could see the water. Blue-green.

In spring all her body grew buds. It was a good spring. She had learnt the hymn of the water; she sang the hymn of the water and her heart was filled with a gradual joy. She gave the feeling of joy to the buds. The leaves were becoming greener and greener.

In summer the water was blue. She could see the fish.

In autumn the cold came. The sky was blue-grey. Her heart was of course filled with the feeling of joy. The heart had assumed the nature of a tree. It accumulated everything.

Midway through winter she fed on human milk. She had a feeling of explosion. Spring had not come yet and the ice was breaking in her entire body. She was in pain. She was filled with a feeling of explosion and she was in pain and she was staring at the water. The water was not flowing any more; it moved drop by drop. The myriad of drops was going, and Mahdokht was in pain. Mahdokht was permeating the water. In the flesh, she recognized the drops of water and the beating of every particle's heart. She fed on human milk for three months. Midway through spring, the tree explosion in her body reached a climax. The explosion was not abrupt; although it was an explosion, it came slowly and gradually. It was as though all her vasculums were about to go to pieces. The vasculums slowly went to pieces, moaning.

Mahdokht was breaking apart in an eternal metamorphosis. She was in pain, she felt like she was giving birth. She was in pain, her eyes were bulging out of their sockets. The water was not even drops any more. It was particles of ether and Mahdokht could see that. Together with the ether, the water was opening up.

Finally it was over. The entire tree had become seeds. A mountain of seeds.

The wind blew. It trusted Mahdokht's seed with the water.

Mahdokht travelled with the water. Travelled in the water. She became a guest to the world. She went all over the world.

MONIRU RAVANIPOUR

Mana, Kind Mana

I said, 'How come you don't know? The sea is full of sharks; sharks that look like fish, so much so that you wouldn't understand unless you get close to them and feel their breath. And in that case, you're already finished.'

He laughed. He was sitting on this very black sofa, across from me, and he was laughing. Then his glance fell on this flowerpot, or perhaps he deliberately wanted to change the subject. He said, 'Your marsh palms are dying. You'd better water them.'

I said, 'Palms in the marsh? No ... I don't like it.'

He pushed back his hair from his forehead. 'You wicked Bushehri!'[1]

He would come; always when he happened to come to Tehran, he would come to my house and we would sit down and read stories and talk.

That day also he had come and we had read stories and now he had to go. It was getting dark and the star – the twinkling star – had come out and sat in the sky, facing the window.

1. Bushehr is a port in southern Iran, on the Persian Gulf coast.

I didn't know where his home was or even what his name was; I was always afraid of knowing his name. Once you know someone's name, he'll separate from you; you've automatically separated him from yourself. And we didn't want that; didn't want to be apart. That's why he didn't know my name, nor I his; we only knew each other and found each other, even if we got lost among all the world's lost people.

'Where's your home?'

'Far away, too far away.'

I asked him once and never again! I was afraid to ask, just as I was afraid to look at him; anxiety tortured me and I said to myself: What if there's no home at all? You can't build a house with the waves of the sea, can you? Always when a twinkling star sat in the sky, he got up, stood by the window and looked at the sky as if he was on the deck of a frigate and the sea was stormy and the night was dark and he was trying to find the course. As if he was searching for a sign, a sign of life.

Then he sighed and went to put on his boots, and if I said, 'Telephone …?' he would say, 'I can't call you from the sea, and you don't have wireless either …'

But this time when he was leaving I said, 'When will you be back?'

It was something that I had never said, and he was lost in thought, and then he turned and pointed at the calligraphy picture he had written for me himself: 'When the seas are aflame.'

I felt cold, a shiver ran down my spine, and he seemed to have realized; he changed the subject again. 'Have pity on this pot; plant something in it, something that you like.' And he left …

For a long time there was the sound of his footsteps and then his diving into water and his hands and how they picked marine plants or the coral branches at the bottom of the sea …

My house was full of things he always brought with him … Colourful shells in which storms howled day and night. Sea animals, starfish and coral branches …

How had I got to know him and where?

It would be useless if I said that words will change everything into an administrative correspondence; this everyone knows and I also know that sometimes you should find a memory, a memory that has been part of your life, in remote times, very remote, before your earthly body could have been formed on earth and move. You find this memory one day, on this very earth, an earth with a virtual crust that, if you are smart and you recognise it, you can understand it with one glance and crack it.

The first time I saw him was a bleak dusk; I was sitting sheltered by the cliffs and I was looking at the sea, which was green, blue and grey ... I couldn't let go; neither of the sea nor of Bushehr. I had come from Tehran, and every day at sunset I came and sat under the sheltering cliffs.

That day I saw there was someone else too, someone standing in a navy uniform; as if paying careful attention to the sound of something, he was listening, facing the sea, as if there was something he couldn't figure out; he came towards me quietly, took his cap off and said, 'Can you hear it too?'

When he sat by me the sun was halfway down in the water, and we were quite familiar and knew each other, but it was as though he didn't know the sea properly; he had just got his ranks and was now about to start his life on the sea.

I said, 'It's the sound of the shellfish ...'

He said, 'Ah ...'

And the shellfish sounded, 'Hooo ... hooo ...', and the sound of the fluttering of the starfish came and the sound of the drying up of the coral branches.

He said, 'Is it always like this? Always at this time, at sunset?'

I said, 'No, there must be something up.'

I said nothing until the shellfish slowly came up with their mother-of-pearl shells and started climbing up my legs and arms. I said, 'One of the blue ones must be sad; you know, the mermaids fall in love as long as they're blue; and now one of them must have fallen in love, fallen in love with a fisherman or ... a sailor perhaps ...' I said, 'I'm leaving, I'm definitely leaving; it's very seldom that they call you from inside the sea, from the depths of green waters ...' He laughed in silence, in his own silence and in the uproar of the sea and the moaning of the shellfish ...

I remember his laughter, the laughter a part of which becomes clear to me as each day passes. Maybe he did know everything and was laughing at me; maybe he was surprised and maybe his laughter was a laughter of homesickness, the laughter of a seaman fallen on land.

We left together; there was me and there was him with his white navy uniform and the small and big shellfish and seaweed that clung to our legs and arms and the starfish that fluttered their colourful arms and wept.

We went so far as to find one of the blue ones shivering and dying of fever. There was tar in her blue hair, her body smelled of oil and her breathing made a rustling sound. Her eyes were half-open and you couldn't bring yourself to look at her; if you looked at her, if you saw those half-open, oil-smeared eyes, you would burst into tears and could not ...

The smell of oil had filled everywhere and the memory of the sea was slowly getting lost in the minds of the blue ones. The blue ones were trembling with fury and turning red before the eyes of that young sailor and me.

I said, 'God, you see? From now on, the sea will always be stormy. The mermaids are turning red.' I said, 'From now on, the sea will always be dark; the moon comes up with the hope of the blue ones, and now look, look yourself ...'

He was silent and he was looking at one of the blue ones that had fever, with tar sticking in her hair, and her body smelling of oil.

I said, 'It's what the sharks have done, this is what the sharks have done.' And I cried, I cried until morning, and when we came out of the water and the sun came up, we were sitting on the cliffs;

I was still crying and he was deep in thought and he feared the blue ones when they cried.

I had said that the crying of the blue ones raised the sea so high that it might drown the port, drown the port of Bushehr.

He was deep in thought and he was sighing and at the bottom of his eyes there was something that I couldn't look at, like the last time when he said in this very house, 'Plant something in your pot, something that you like.'

When it was going to happen, right at that moment, I was here, in Tehran, in this very flat, number forty, fourth floor, down Qaitarriyyeh Park ... The building was rocking, as if it was a frigate on the sea; the doors and the walls were going to pieces as if the building was the hull of a frigate hit by laser-guided missiles; the plant pots in the flat were rocking, picture frames fell from the walls and I could hear shouts, queer shouts, and by now I knew that the sharks had set everything on fire in the process of chewing the sea. Neither the radio nor the television said anything; such words always drop dead by the time they get to me, and their carcasses fall around me. There is always a smell around me, the smell of the carcasses of dead and rotten words; words that have struggled, struggled for years to reach me and they have never done.

I received the news in a different way; when the water came up under my window on the fourth floor, and the crying shellfish and starfish reached me, I heard moans that were not earthly moans. I know the moans of land people: they are dusty and drawn, they are black, they smell of the staleness of history; they are disturbed and devastating like a whirlwind; the moan was the moan of the blue ones; was the groan of the sea duck through which, through its crystalline smooth pain and sorrow, you could see the moon turning red, turning dark.

'Hooo ... hooo ...'

I got up and drew the curtains; everywhere the seawater was coming up, the green seawater; and the trees of Qaitarriyyeh were drowning in the water, and the shellfish were coming in through every window and crawling up the doors and walls of the house.

And then when I saw her – the mermaid that had become lean, and had cried so much that there were hollows under her eyes, and her blue body ripped apart by laser beam – I realised that it was true; that everything that had to have happened on the other side had happened. I reached out my hand through the mesh fence of the balcony; the wave of the sea hit me in the face; my breath was choking; the waves of the sea were rising up to the rooftop; I hugged the blue one that was lean and breathing painstakingly, and she sat on the same black sofa, the same sofa on which a young sailor had sat one day; she sat there and cried …

The sea seemed to have caught fire. Shellfish, coral and the mermaid were moaning in my house and the seagulls were flying over the city with their sorrowful scream. And I wanted to see him, his childish smile, his large lemon-shaped eyes, his long thin cheeks and his hair that was smooth and he sometimes pushed it back from his forehead with his hand … But were was he?

The fish that were fish, and the smell of their breath which was the smell of fish, small and big; they came in through the widows, the stairs and the door; the pot of the marsh palm was rocking and the dried-up stems had been rooted out and then I saw, I saw with my very eyes, that a small sillago fish had put his eyes in the pot; eyes that were large and lemon-shaped and always used to stare at the star, the twinkling star.

When the sea water receded, when the mermaid calmed down and went to grow old with her sorrow, I was left with a large ceramic vase and earth that smelled of the salty sea and a sea that was full of sharks and sharks that were on the land.

Zohreh Hatami

Grandmother

Massoumeh was shedding tears as she followed her mother's every step from the storeroom to the room and from the room to the courtyard. She wished she could untie her mother's bundle, take the *chador* off her head and tell her that she could stay in this house forever. Tell her, 'This house is yours; it's my duty to be your walking stick when you're old.' She wished she could tell her, 'As long as I breathe I'll be your obedient slave. For God's sake don't be so sad. Don't think so hard.' Tell her …

Massoumeh was sitting in the doorway looking at the sun that looked as if it didn't want to jump down the edge of the wall. She heard the intermittent sound of her mother's shuffling steps on the stairs. She went up the stairs, came down, stopped. She panted and started again. She looked as if she had lost something.

Perhaps it wasn't six months yet. Massoumeh had gone to his brother's house to bring her mother. Calm and patient, mother was collecting her possessions. She was going up and coming down the stairs. Massoumeh stood waiting outside the house door. She was extremely furious. She had heard from neighbours that Parvaneh had thrown her mother out of the house several times. Neighbours had taken her to their houses. She was thinking that before her mother became disabled, how respected she had been and how she had always observed courtesy with the neighbours. She always said that a person with dignity should not pour out her heart to everyone.

Her mother kept going up and coming down the stairs, and Massoumeh was standing by the door. Parvaneh had gone into the room and didn't show up. On that day Massoumeh had said aloud, 'I spit on my brother's pride! If he were a man, he wouldn't have thrown her mother under the claws of a Godforsaken witch like you. That miserable excuse for a man hasn't got a wife; he's got a husband!'

And she had said to her brother and his wife whatever swear words she knew. Then she had slammed the door so hard that her own body had shaken from the bang. A long while later, in the public bath she had seen blue patches on her mother's body. The old woman had said stuttering, 'It's because of menopause, dear.' For three months on end, Massoumeh had boycotted her sister-in-law and refused to visit her brother's house. However, during the bathing ceremony following her own recent birth-giving, they greeted each other lukewarmly once their glances met, and by the afternoon everything was forgotten.

Now her mother was going back to the same house and Massoumeh had no choice. Her heart was laden with sorrow. She knew that her mother couldn't stay in that house any more. The night when she had brought her home, her husband had knotted his brows. Massoumeh had been anxious. She had paid attention to all details. She had cooked the meal her husband liked best. She gave him the towel as always. She poured tea for him and hung his clothes on the coat hanger. She stretched a blanket for him to sit on and went to prepare the dinner. She did all these things with so much sycophancy that it made the man more pertinacious. Her husband was in a bad mood and none of Massoumeh's deeds had any moderating effect. Her mother was sitting in the corner of the room, putting *halva*[1] into her grandchildren's mouths with her finger. The husband was peering at her wet finger out of the corner of his eye. Massoumeh knew that when her husband became pertinacious he wouldn't calm down until he ejected his venom. She thought of reciting '*amman yujib*'[2] five times to shut her husband's mouth.

'Oh God, have mercy. Please do something so that his temper will be quenched and no mishap follows.'

She started to recite the prayer. She recited it three times; she had just begun to recite it for the fourth time when the glass of water slipped out of Ahmad's little hand. Massoumeh saw the flowing strips of water crawling towards her husband's plate. The man's hand went up and hit hard at the back of Ahmad's hand. Ahmad burst out crying. He sulked and went away from the spread. The husband burst out shouting. Massoumeh glanced at her mother. Ahmad was the apple of her eyes. Massoumeh feared that her mother would interfere. Mother got up. She took Ahmad's hand and yanked him towards the spread.

'Kids shouldn't sulk if dad tells them off. Get up, get up and come here and have your dinner, otherwise there'll be no stories tonight.'

Ahmad sat by grandmother, frowning. Grandmother filled the glass with water again and handed it to him. 'Grip it fast and be careful it doesn't fall. Anyone who sulks at the dinner table, Satan will enter his body.'

Her husband said nothing more and started to eat. He wasn't a bad-tempered man, but he had loose hands. When he got angry he beat up Massoumeh or the kids. He would regret it afterwards; he would squirm in a corner and keep silent. And the day after, he would come home with arms full of fruit packets. But his temper had got worse since the old women had come to their house. As a matter of fact, the reason for his violence was no more his being

---

1. A sweet dessert dish made from flour, saffron, ghee and rosewater.
2. Reference to a Koranic verse recited traditionally in times of distress and despair, imploring mercy from God: "Who listens to the distressed when he calls on Him, and Who relieves his suffering, and makes you (mankind) inheritors of the earth? (Can there be another) god besides Allah? Little it is that ye heed!" (*an-Naml*, verse 62)

angry or tired or the kids being noisy. He beat up the kids without any reason. If Massoumeh went forward, she would also be beaten up. It was as though he wanted to drive her mother crazy. As if he wanted to tell her mother, 'Since you've set foot in this house everything has been screwed up.'

When she tried to mediate they would end up quarrelling. Last night amid the argument, her husband blew his top, 'What business of hers is it to intervene in our life? I know better how to treat my kid. She'd spoilt these two so much that you can't tell them anything. They can't be controlled any more. I don't want to see Ahmad become like her worthless son. If she knew how to raise kids, she wouldn't have raised her own son in a way that he'd become a slave to his wife.'

Massoumeh and her husband went to their room. Her husband continued shouting. Massoumeh had burst out crying and she covered her mouth with the corner of the quilt and sobbed. Her husband smoked cigarettes relentlessly, walked around the room and swore at her brother and mother. He said, 'What have I done? Her blockhead son is mooning about and I have to bear the burden of his old woman.'

Massoumeh said, 'But I'm also her daughter. He's kept her for several years; it's our turn for some time.'

Her husband yelled, 'When I married you, you didn't tell me that there was also an old bitch in the deal. Huh, did you?'

Tears were running down Massoumeh's face. 'She's not an old bitch. She's my mother. Please speak quieter.'

'She's also the mother of that worthless thickhead. It's his duty, not mine. The good-for-nothing jackass has thrown her mother out for us to suffer.'

'It's not my brother's fault. You know well that it's his heartless wife who's lit this fire.'

'What's the damn difference? Even when she's here, for months on end he won't come to check if his old woman's dead or alive. Still this ungrateful old woman loves him more than you.'

'Well, he's her older son. I wasn't even sixteen when I left her home. He's been with her all his life.'

'She's only brought her bragging to us. If he's so dear to her, okay, then let her go to him so that when she kicks the bucket one of theses days, her beloved son ties the handkerchief under her chin. The ungrateful hag keeps eating my bread and supporting him.'

Massoumeh clung to her husband's legs.

When Massoumeh got up at the call for morning prayers, she saw her mother sitting with her head on her knee. It seemed that she hadn't slept all night. Massoumeh felt that her mother had heard all the talking. She knew that after last night's words, her mother would no more sit at her son-in-law's spread and would quietly leave. In the morning, after her husband left, her mother busied herself with everyday work. Massoumeh was watching her. It seemed that since last night her back had bent more and the wrinkles of her face had multiplied. She hardly stole a glance at Massoumeh and did not cross her path. Massoumeh had busied herself in the kitchen but her mind was with her mother. Her mother kept going up and down the stairs. With those crippled legs, she went to the pool and washed her hands. She got up again and walked towards the stairs. She knew that she had to go; she was hesitating. It was as if she wished Massoumeh would stop her and tell her that she would keep her at any price. In the end, she went to the corner of the yard. She sat under the sun and started undoing her grey braids. Her wooden comb was moving in the water bowl next to her. The sun shone on her face.

Massoumeh's husband had said he would go to her brother's shop on his way. She wanted her mother to be ready before the brother arrived. But it was as if her mother didn't intend to go. She neither collected her possessions nor packed her bundle. From the kitchen, Massoumeh looked at her bony figure and her grey, henna-dyed hair. After the death of their father, her mother had suffered much to raise her and her brother. A thought passed her mind: 'How my mother's changed. She's changed so much.' She couldn't stay in the kitchen any more. She went into the courtyard and sat facing her.

'Mother, I wanted to say that ...'

But her voice broke. Mother was just staring at her. Then she turned her gaze from her face and said, 'My poor Sepideh is very lonely during the day. I must go and see her.'

Massoumeh looked down.

'It's only for a while. When he cools down I'll be back ...'

She started sobbing. Mother weaved a strand of hair she had undone and combed, and didn't touch the other strand. She put her scarf on. She got up and started collecting her possessions. She was trying not to look at Massoumeh and not to show her reproach. She tied the ten tooman bill Massoumeh had given her in the corner of the headscarf and said, 'Parvaneh is not such a bad girl. If I wash the dishes at night and don't leave them for the morning ... I say, dear, don't forget to give me some of that cough syrup to take with me. I cough a little at nights. When I cough Parvaneh ...'

Massoumeh said, 'You've finished your syrup. I'll take you to the doctor next week. Perhaps he'll give you something better for your chest.'

'Oh no, dear. Last year he gave me something as bitter as the snake's tail. I kept throwing up phlegm. Parvaneh hated me even more. This syrup is all right. Get some more of the same for me.'

'Okay, mother.'

The doorbell rang. It was Reza. She stepped aside so that the brother would come in.

'Hello, brother. Welcome. Please come inside.'

"I beg of you, sister. I was having a row with Parvaneh just now. She sulked and left for her mother's. Sepideh's been left on my hands. I've left her with the neighbours. I was wondering if you could do something for me. If you could just keep mother here for a few more weeks so that I may convince Parvaneh.'

'Brother, I swear to Fatemeh[1] that I'd keep her if only I could. Akbar Aqa said he'd divorce me if he comes back and sees mother here. You know how stubborn he is.'

---

1. Prophet Muhammad's daughter and only offspring, and wife of first Shi'i Imam Ali, considered an infallible saint by Iranian Shi'ites.

'What am I supposed to do? I've kept her a lifetime. You and your husband couldn't keep her even for six months.'

'Brother, you know that I'm not in charge of my life. Please take her so that later when he cools off, I can come and take her back. Don't worry about Parvaneh. With the kind of mother she's got, she won't survive there one single day.'

Her brother sat on the stair and didn't say anything any more.

'Let's go into the room, brother. Why are you sitting here? It's not nice.'

'No, it's okay here. I have to go. I have a thousand miseries to attend to. I've left work to come here.'

Massoumeh left and came back with a plate of pastries. Ahmad and Maryam went to their uncle. He kissed their faces and picked pastries from the plate and put them in their mouth.

Ahmad said, 'Uncle, have you come to take granny with you?'

Grandmother's voice rose from the room's doorway, 'May God take my life instead of yours. Thanks for coming, dear. I wanted to come myself.'

'Hello, mother. Are you ready?'

'Hello my dear. Have something, dear. Make your mouth sweet.'

Massoumeh said, 'What's the rush, now? For God's sake have something, brother.'

Her brother took a cookie and got up. 'Get up, mother. Let's go.'

Mother clambered up with great difficulty. She wobbled on her handicapped legs. Massoumeh held her arm and handed her bundle to her.

Massoumeh stood by the front door and watched them as they disappeared from sight beyond the alley's bend.

'Did you see that she finally didn't finish the story of Moon-face?'

Maryam put down the half-eaten pastry she had lifted to her mouth, looked at the plate of pastries and said, 'Yeah, I wish she had stayed one more night.'

FARKHONDEH AQAEI

The Little Secret

Vaji pulled the blanket up to her chest. She pursed her lips and curled herself up. The pain was intensifying, the pain that started from the feet, crawled up and peaked at the abdominal region. The woman clawed at her stomach. Cold sweat soaked her body. She got goose pimples. She gave out an exhausted, drawn breath. Her mouth was dry and tasted awful. Painstakingly she lifted the glass and swallowed a gulp. The cool water touched her lips and went down her parched and hot throat. She dropped herself on the pillow. Now the pain had gone; comfortable and relaxed, as if she had not been squirming a moment earlier. She shut her eyes and heard the calm, continuous voice of a boy who was whispering amorously.

'I'll be so upset if you don't come tomorrow. For heaven's sake, do come tomorrow. I miss you so. It's so straightforward. You come to the station. You get the Hassan Abad bus. When you get off in the square, it's ten minutes' walk. Anybody will show you the place immediately if you ask. Then you come to the fourth floor, women's ward. Well, don't tell them. You'll pretend you're going to school. Come on. Okay, don't come alone. Come with a friend of yours. I say, why don't you come with Azam? Where's Azam? Let me talk to her. There's no reason to be ashamed. Why's she ashamed? We're to become relatives eventually. You know what? I've got something to tell her. Whatever! Don't be cross. I just want to thank her for taking my letters to you. She's a real pal. Happy the one who falls in love with her. Not everyone is like you. It's two months I've been here. Neither a phone call nor a message. I'll be waiting for you tomorrow. No more excuses …'

The man's voice had no end for Vaji. She knew that she would hear it as long as she listened. She got up. She closed the door and went back to bed. She pulled the quilt over her head and went to sleep. During these two months, days had always started too early in the hospital. The night nurse, with tired red-rimmed eyes, shook the thermometer in the air, put it in the patient's mouth and left. The next nurse came with a notebook.

'Have your bowels moved?'

She took notes. She removed the thermometer and looked. She made a note and left. The next nurse came with a urine vessel. She looked at the numbers on the beds and gave urine vessels to some of the patients and left. The next nurse came with a basket full of syringes, looked at her notebook and went to the beds:

'Pull your sleeve up!'

She tied the tourniquet tightly round the arm and prepared the syringe:

'How many days you been here? How many kids do you have? A baby girl is a good omen. I myself have got two. Which day's your operation? Finished.'

And she put the blood-filled syringe in the basket and left. The head nurse came with a moveable tray full of bottles of pills and capsules. For each patient she dropped one, two or three pills in a paper cup and put it on the table.

'Well, swallow it! You better swallow it while I'm here. I've heard you don't take your pills. Are you making a saving?'

Then a nurse brought the ampoules and then it was the cleaner's turn to sweep the floor and wipe it with gunny sack, and after her came a different cleaner with sponge and detergent powder and cleaned the washbasin in the room, and then a woman wiped the closet and the windowpanes with a moist cloth and dumped the dried out flowers and washed her cloth, and after she left, Mohammad Aqa put the breakfast tray on the bed table. The ward supervisor reported on the beds in a loud voice, handing them over to the day shift supervisor and left, and then everything was as the day before, with new people who kept coming and going in the morning and evening and night.

Vaji picked up the teacup and came out of the room. Her roommate was combing her hair. Vaji knew that if she hesitated another moment, her roommate would get up and fill the room with the acrid and repugnant smell of toothpaste. Although work had begun in the ward, patients who had the strength to walk hadn't got up yet. Vaji sat down in the corridor on the sofa by the window. Hassan Azarmi, the patient in the next room, was the first one who had had his breakfast and was coming with his walking stick to sit next to Vaji. It was a long time now that they saw each other every day. Azarmi said hello under his breath and sat next to her, facing the elevator. He lit his cigarette. He ran his hand over the bandage on his eye. This was a movement he made every few minutes, as if he wanted to make sure that the bandage was still there. Vaji was not in the mood for Azarmi, with that cigarette always dangling from the corner of his lip, the smoke of which made Vaji sick. As always, she opened the window and sat with her back to Azarmi. When Azarmi lit up his second cigarette, Vaji got up and went to her room. The doctors came at nine.

'How are you feeling today?'

'I'm better, but last night I had a fever and I was shivering again.'

'Didn't the nurse give you a painkiller?'

'No, I didn't ask for it. But, doctor, you said I'd become better after the operation.'

'Evidently. But this pain is because of the wound and the stitches. At midday today we have a council meeting about you. After the meeting we'll decide about the method of treatment and the medication.'

'Is it dangerous?'

'No – a small tumour the size of an egg. We'll talk about it in more detail later if necessary.'

The doctor had gone to deal with Vaji's roommate who had a kidney disease. Vaji reached her hand under the sheet and squeezed her belly. The tumour seemed to her to be larger than an egg. It was perhaps the size of a round, stuffed ball that had become hard and rigid. Her roommate was sitting by the window:

'Doctor says I'll be discharged.'

'Lucky you.'

'Don't be upset. You'll also be discharged soon.'

'Yeah.' And she counted on her thin yellow fingers: five, six, seven. This was the seventh person who had shared the room with her; she was leaving now, while Vaji's situation was still not clear.

'I'm going to the room at the end of the corridor. Everyone's there. Won't you come?'

'I'll come later.'

The woman was gone. Vaji thought, 'Mrs Amini was my first roommate, and now the seventh one is leaving. Mrs Amini had cancer. In her breast. Her left breast. She was a nurse herself. How come she hadn't noticed it? She'd been hospitalised for two months.' Vaji had come lately. And a week later Mrs Amini had died. Vaji thought, 'Mine isn't cancer. Two months have gone by and I'm feeling well, I just have a fever and shivering and pain sometimes. It's not unnatural after an operation. Everyone gets it.'

And she touched the egg in her belly. No, it was larger. The doctor was wrong; although they'd taken one-kilogram tumours out of the bellies of some patients. The doctor had said, 'A small cyst, a one-hour operation.' And now the cyst was still there although they'd opened her belly.

'There's nothing wrong with me, I know it.'

She listened. From among all the mingled and crowded voices, Azarmi's quiet voice could be heard.

'Why didn't you come, my dear one? How long I've been staring at the door! I'll finally make you pay for these days. You'll see. I've been waiting since morning. I had prepared pastries and fruits thinking that now Ashraf Khanom will come. She'll come in a minute. In a minute. In a couple of minutes ... You're too cruel. I emptied a pack of cigarettes. You needn't worry about my cigarettes; I'll somehow get some. Last night I was dreaming of you till morning. I was sure you'd come. Visiting hours aren't in the morning evidently. Nevertheless I went downstairs at half-past six and notified the guards. They're nice kids. I told them to bring you to me if you came from school. You only had to mention my name. Why? The doctor came. Said they'd undo the bandage on my left eye in a couple of days. Never mind. One eye's better than none at all. I shouldn't have called you. But I couldn't help it. I thought maybe you'd come and not found me. Not knowing that you didn't care at all ...'

There was a sound of two nurses laughing: 'She's ditched him again!'

The head nurse yelled, 'Mr Azarmi! Mr Azarmi! Be a little considerate. It's two hours now that Dr Sedaqat has been waiting in line.'

'Okay sister, okay. Well then. I'll call and talk properly at night. So long.'

The nurse asked, 'Didn't come today either?'

'No, but she'll come tomorrow. I'll encourage her.'

Vaji thought she was lucky not to have a telephone at home and that her daughter was not involved in such affairs. She hated Azarmi's obstinate attitude.

Her body grew hot gradually. The pain slowly crawled up the legs and reached her stomach. She crumpled up into a ball. She knew that a moment later it would make her helpless. With all her strength she raised her body and rang the bell. And before the nurse injected the painkiller she had passed out.

When Vaji opened her black swollen eyes, a cool breeze was blowing through the window and at her body. In the dim light of the lamp coming from the corridor, another bed was empty. Through the gaping of the door, the large round desk of the nurses was visible. One of the nurses was sitting, drowsing with knitting needles in her hand. Two chairs were put together and another nurse was sleeping on them. Vaji got up. She felt a little pain in her abdominal region. She took up her *chador* and wrapped it round her. The nurse was furtively watching her walk slowly and sluggishly. Noone was around, not even Hassan Azarmi. The black and silent telephone was dangling against the wall. Vaji wondered since what time she'd been sleeping. Was it midday or afternoon? She couldn't remember. She thought her husband and Farrokh must have come when she was asleep. She sat by the window. Maybe they hadn't come. She would have woken up if they had come. She got up and went back into the room. She switched on the light. A packet of fruit was on the bedside table. So they had come when she was asleep. Was it her husband Mokhtar who had come or Farrokh? Or both? What had they done with Reza? The little cute Reza who was two years old. Farrokh had said, 'Don't worry, I'll take care of him.'

But what could a young girl do? She counted. Fifteen, seventeen – she was eighteen. Her young smiling eyes sparkled in her moonlit face framed by the *chador*. The black *chador* suited her. It accentuated the whiteness and roundness of her face. 'Mom, don't worry. Reza's got used to it. He sometimes doesn't remember at all.'

So life was going on without her too. Calmly. Like the afternoons, when she wasn't there and everyone else was there. Everything was in its place. She shuddered. The little anxiety that was in her body was rising. Her heart ached. Mrs Amini had also been hospitalised for two months. Then she had died. Although she was a nurse herself. How come she hadn't realised that she had cancer? She used to walk in the corridor every afternoon. With her hands under her armpits, she sometimes fondled her left breast gently. Never mind. She was no different from those who were going to be dismissed tomorrow. She was just a little thinner and a little more yellow. And one morning Mrs Amini was gone. Without Vaji having talked to her. When she died, everyone said, 'She had cancer.' Vaji thought, 'Mine isn't cancer. I would've realised it if it were. It's not.' First the pain would come once a week, and then she didn't have any pain till next week. But why was it that after the operation she was having pain every night, and why wouldn't it leave her alone even during the days? The following morning the doctor was by her bed.

'This is all illusion and fear. The day before yesterday, we discussed your case in the council. First we'd diagnosed the tumour to be in the uterus and that we'd remove it with a simple operation; but in the operating room, we found that it was a benign tumour in the stomach and intestine area. Of course we did an biopsy, and for that reason we couldn't have a clear conclusion till this morning. But rest assured from now on. The council decided not to have another operation on you. We'll treat you with chemotherapy and medication in a few months.'

'When can I go home?'

'Whenever you wish. In my view, you had better stay here. We can take better care of you here.'

Azarmi's voice could be heard: 'God bless this wonderful mother-in-law. She's really so nice. You did right to ask for her permission to come. If only you knew how great I was feeling yesterday. After you left, I was thinking of you all the time. To be honest, I didn't think that you'd come. Yesterday morning, the guys from the neighbourhood had come. Your brother was here too. No, don't be scared. You should've seen it; they brought loads of fruit and nuts and cigarettes. I say, Ashraf, you've become so thin! What are you worrying about? Really? Never mind. Believe me, walking with the stick is a lot of fun. Please come tomorrow too. Come and let me see you more. This time you must come into my room. Why are you embarrassed? Aren't we engaged? It's not nice in the garden, you know. Yes, I saw those two women. Was she really your mother? Why didn't you say so? I noticed that she was looking at us a lot. But she was holding her *chador* too tight. I couldn't recognise her. You should've introduced her. There was so much fruit and pastries upstairs and you left without eating anything. Your mother's very kind. I love her after you. You won't get upset, will you? I've told my mother and my relatives not to come here except on Fridays so that you can come here comfortably. I'll be waiting for you tomorrow. Okay, the day after. This time you should come into my room. I'll be upset if you don't. Stay by the phone. When these few people finish calling, I'll ring you. So long.'

Vaji thought that there was no end to this man's talk. She wished the telephone were not behind her room's wall. All the time ringing, words, small talk, how are you. What other business is there to have with a patient except asking how he is? Vaji thought that if she were in the shoes of Ashraf's mother, she would not come nor would she let her daughter come. Then she leaned over to see Azarmi going, walking stick in hand, dragging his leg behind him.

So Ashraf had come. When she had been sleeping. I would've seen her if I'd been awake. Farrokh had come too, but I'd passed out. Azarmi's right to be hopeful, but how about me?

Nahid's voice was coming from the end of the corridor. Now she must have half-risen on her bed, waving her black, thin arms in the air, yelling with a thick Dezfuli accent.

'I'm not hitting out at you who are listening; they call this the capital, meaning that people of other towns should be homeless and vagrant. Their youth should go to face the bullets so that these chosen ones can live in comfort and have no troubles, walk down the streets with their noses in the air. You conscienceless people! Day and night they're pouring bombs on us from the earth and the sky, and we don't utter a word. But as soon as you step in here, it's as if there's no war. Once a year or month, when they make the sirens wail for the fun of it, these wretched bastards go hide in the deepest hole. Aren't you ashamed? I wish to God you all become sterile! Let go of me. You're breaking my arm. You pimps! I didn't say anything blasphemous, did I?'

And her struggling voice choked in her throat. And a few moments later, a woman removed the jars from the bed trays with her thick hands and with much noise, and took her red bowl to the small, slippery ice slabs and poured ice water in the jars. And now a woman who had a bandage on her nose was looking at Vaji.

'Did you have an operation?'

'Yes.'

'Is it hard?'

'No, the hard part is the coming to.'

When the ward telephone rang, Vaji wasn't paying attention to her roommate any more, because a moment later all the nurses were in motion, almost running. Vaji could see through the door their coming and going, but she realised the reason for all the excitement only when the loudspeaker started playing military music. She came out of the room. Almost all the patients were standing in the corridor and gazing. The stretchers were being taken downstairs by the elevator. Collapsible beds and dusty mattresses were being taken out of the storage room. Two people unfolded the beds and put the mattresses on them and another one wiped them with a piece of cloth. The loudspeakers of the ward were giving out military music and the latest news from the battlefront. Two cleaners accompanied by a medic went to the rooms. The head nurse's commanding voice was loud. The voice of Mrs Nasseri, the ward's head nurse, was the only constant sound continuously heard everyday from seven in the morning to two in the afternoon. Now she was issuing orders:

'Pull this bed closer, push that one farther back. Okay, now bring that collapsible one here and put it between them.'

'Well, dear ma'am, I know you're ill, but please be a little more cooperative. It's war; it's out of my hands. Faster, yes, also take your belongings into that room.'

Vaji thought that it was the best time for her to change her room. She took her clothes out of the wardrobe. Nasseri's voice rose:

'No, Mrs Vassel, you stay right in that room. We want to keep a close eye on you. Aqa Habib, help them bring that wardrobe out, so that the bed will fit in.'

'Mr Azarmi, what on earth are you doing in here? You better go to the phone and not block our way so much.'

'Okay, it's okay now. So far we've placed all the women in this part of the ward. The other half is for brothers.'

The sound of ambulance sirens from the street blurred Mrs Nasseri's sound, as well as the sound from the loudspeakers, and an hour later, one extra bed was introduced into every double bedroom, and the three-bed rooms had become five-bedders. The sides of the corridor were full of beds on each of which lay a young – or seldom old – man, and although it was an hour before visiting time, the rooms were full of crowds standing over their patients, weeping and moaning. In the corridor, some people were massaging the shoulders of a fainted woman. The tables were heaped up with bouquets of flowers and boxes of pastries. Vaji thought, 'How have they got wind of this so quickly?' From the operating room, patients were still coming out. It was past two, but Mrs Nasseri's voice could still be heard. Air-conditioners and fans were working at full steam. The windows were open, but a warm, choking air had filled the rooms.

Mokhtar had come alone, and later Vaji's mother came too. She stood by Vaji's bed. Some people had come from Dezful to visit Nahid, who was now Vaji's roommate. A few people were also standing over the bandaged face.

Vaji was short of breath. 'Let's go into the garden.'

'Would it be all right for you?'

'Sure, it's quite useful for me.'

Ignoring the pain that squeezed her stomach, Vaji put on her *chador* and made her way to the garden through the dense crowd that constantly moved to and fro. Mokhtar was calm, but whenever his glance fell on Vaji, his upper lip twanged.

'Hasn't Farrokh come?'

'No, she had homework.'

'Doctor said there's no need for operation.'

'Told me so as well.'

'When did he talk to you?'

'Yesterday, when we were here. You were asleep. Doctor had stayed to talk to me. How many times did I tell you to go to the doctor sooner? You wouldn't. You let it go too far.'

'Don't start again. There's nothing wrong with me now. I'm only weak. I want to go home.'

'Why?'

'What do you mean?'

'Nothing. I mean are you uncomfortable here? Don't they take care of you?'

'I miss Reza. They keep bringing the wounded here every day. They're in need of beds. There's nothing wrong with me except that I've occupied one man's place.'

'Stay here and rest for a week or two. At home Reza will disturb you and get on your nerves.'

'I want to come home just for his sake.'

'On the contrary, it's better for him not to see you, because he's got used to it now. If you come back home and then you're supposed to return to hospital, he'll get restless.'

Vaji looked at her mother, who was all ears, not uttering a word.

'Mother, please you say something.'

Her mother stared at Vaji. Tears had welled up in her eyes. With a quiet, choked voice she said, 'You better not come home. Stay and rest for a week.'

An hour later, when Vaji was back in the room, a cleaner was mopping the floor. Nahid was showing her burnt legs and talking to herself, 'When my legs heal, I'll leave. Anywhere I go will be better than here. I hate this place. I hated it from the beginning. I used to come once a year or in a few months to see my relatives. Now I don't want to come any more.'

Vaji took her *chador* off and lay on the bed. She knew that if she said a single word, Nahid would begin pouring out her heart. Nahid stared at the woman who was looking at her with two eyes through a bandage on her face. Her dark brown face turned blue. She slapped her knees hard with her hands, 'God hates me. He fixed it so that I'd be trapped in this hell again. They failed to treat me in Dezful. Oh, dear God, don't leave anyone at the mercy of mean people. I'm not hitting out at you here; but most of these uptowners are infidels. May God ruin their homes over their heads. They don't have any faith, they don't believe in God. O, God, would it be that the airplanes come and bombard here someday? What's it now? Why have you gathered again? Am I lying? As soon as there's a siren, those wishy-washy women jump into the arms of their husbands. Aren't we women too? My kid's so scared of the sound of rockets and airplanes that he's pissed in his pants at the food spread a dozen times. You don't put on a headscarf. You're too damn proud. Our youth are getting martyred in thousands. Youths as beautiful as flowers go and never come back. But you're too damn proud. You bitches! Let go of me. Let go of my arms. It hurts. No zealous man is around any more. If I had my way, I'd know how to deal with them all. The country's in ruins and these godless yuppies are sleeping like babies.'

Now the patients have gathered at the room's door and the nurse has injected the painkiller, but it hasn't taken effect yet. The woman's voice resonates in the ward:

'Strangle me. Kill me. I'm just like the others. Her shirt collar is open down to her navel and she's got a lace scarf on her head. I'll tear her apart myself. Just let me get hold of her! It's plain cheekiness. O God, God, hear me. What sin did I commit? What was this misery that you cast on me? While everyone else is dying of mortar shells, this wretched soul has to die of boiling water! Tough luck.'

And now the head nurse is standing over Nahid. The woman is crying and beating on her head.

'What? What's the matter ma'am? Why are you hollering? Have

you taken your painkiller? Okay, go to sleep. You'll be discharged in two days. Every single day you've been making a big noise. Your nerves are wrecked. But everyone's nerves are wrecked. Nurse, stay beside her. Call me if she wants to yell.'

She had not left the room yet when Nahid said, 'She's also one of them.'

'What did you say?'

'I said it's nobody's fault. It's all because of the water. Anyone who drinks the water in this place goes nuts.'

'Quiet! You started again?'

The patients had not dispersed yet. Despite all the pain, she came out of the room. She didn't want to be there. In the next room, by the window, Azarmi was sitting in his bed half-crouched, eating pistachios. A young man with a bandaged shoulder was lying on his back, groaning. Next to him, a middle-aged man was sleeping with closed eyes, surrounded by a woman who was seemingly his wife, as well as several young girls and boys. His left arm was in plaster and a weight was connected to his feet from below the bed. The man was silently squeezing a branch of narcissus in his right hand, at times lifting it and smelling at it. The janitor had arrived to push the visitors out, and now with the walking stick in one hand, Azarmi was dragging a chair with his other hand to sit by the phone. Vaji thought, he'll start babbling right away. And she walked to the end of the corridor to stay by the window. A woman standing beside her was blowing kisses with her hand towards the street. A four- or five-year-old child was perched on his father's shoulder, laughing. Why didn't Mokhtar bring Reza to see her and wave his hand for her?

'Sister! Sister!' An old Arab man lying on a fold-up bed with an IV tucked into his forearm was saying in Persian with difficulty, 'My arm, my arm hurts, sister. The needle inside my arm hurts.'

The man's right arm, to which the IV was attached, had swollen. Vaji went back to call the nurse.

'Not that I don't like to see you, but if you can't do it, I won't insist. I miss you so much. Sometimes I'd like to come to you myself. I'm fed up. No, they're nice kids, they care a lot, especially the nurses. But you know, we're not talking about one or two days here. And in the women's ward, of all places. Doctor says it will take time to treat my eye. I'm in no hurry, but, well, I'm more worried about you. Nothing. Just like that. I got upset to hear you didn't have a good exam. It's all my fault. But I'll make it up to you. Never mind! When I get out of here, I'll work with you every day. You'll definitely pass. No, I still have the lessons in my mind; one look and I'll remember them all. I'm so lucky to hear your voice at least. I have a roommate who's come from Bostan; he's been hit in the shoulder by a bullet. He just loves the province. There's also an old man who's gone to pieces and a herd of people are always around him. Not that I'm jealous, but I'd be so happy if you could come. Now you've got no more lessons. I know you'll have retakes, but it's all right, we'll make it.'

'Cut it short, brother, you're drilling our brains.' It was the voice of one of the young men hospitalised in the corridor.

Azarmi was still talking and the cleaner was bringing the food tray and Nahid was sleeping there snoring loudly and the bandage-face woman was looking at herself in the mirror. The pain had slowly started from the feet. Vaji knew that it would then crawl higher and higher and curl up in her stomach. She pushed the emergency button. 'Nurse, painkiller please.'

'What for?'

'The pain's begun.'

When the nurse pulled the empty syringe out of Vaji's flesh, Nahid the Dezfuli, the bandage-face, the food tray, Azarmi's words, the black phone dangling from the wall, the constant ringing, the swollen arm, the narcissus and the groaning of the young man had all faded away.

Vaji had clenched her hands on her stomach, squeezing that big egg which didn't resemble an egg in any real sense. Silence had filled the hospital and Vaji could only hear the regular trickling of the water tap with her eyes closed, and then she couldn't hear that either.

And Mokhtar, cheerful and calm, had put Reza on his shoulder, and Reza was blowing kisses for his mother and waving his hands to come to her arms. Vaji was far away, so far away that despite all her yearning she didn't even reach out her hand to hug him. Farrokh had come with that black demur *chador* of hers to take Reza from Mokhtar's shoulder and hug him, as a mother would, and to cover him with her black *chador*, and Reza was wriggling underneath the *chador* and Farrokh was taking her away, and Mokhtar was looking at her without saying anything. Now Reza wasn't there, Farrokh wasn't there and Mokhtar's shadow was diluted and replaced by the constant trickling of the water tap. Vaji opened her eyes. Nahid had ducked her head under the sheet, and the bandage-face didn't even have those two hazel eyes to look at Vaji. Vaji's dry and bitter mouth irritated her. She got up. The pain whirled in her back. She put on her headscarf and came into the corridor. Beds were put head to tail in the corridor. All the lights were out but one. In the adjacent room the middle-aged man had shoved the plastic narcissus flowers into his nostril and gone to sleep. In the corridor a young man was smoking on his bed. When he heard the sound of Vaji's footsteps, he turned his face to the wall. The smoke from his cigarette hit the wall and ricocheted and thinned out. Both his legs were cut off. The bottom of his sheet was so flat it was as if he had never had legs. The rest of the young men were fast asleep. Bags were scattered on the bedside tables by their heads or under their beds beside packets of fruit and pastries and cans. The old Arab man was holding the IV stand in hand, standing by the window and watching the sleeping city. Although her head felt heavy, Vaji still wanted to walk. Coming out of the room, she was no more thinking of Reza or Farrokh or Mokhtar. Coughing, vomit, fever and shuddering, the one who was throwing up blood, the cigarette that was being lit, the moaning out of pain, the bell that woke up the nurse with a start – they were all there.

But then it was still the silence that continued until the night shift ended and its staff handed everything, neat and orderly, over to those on the day shift. And then the nurses would come again with tired and red-rimmed eyes, with thermometers, urine vessels, blood syringes, tubes of pills and ampoules in their hands, and then the servants came with brooms, sponges, moist cloths and dried-up flowers that had to be discarded. Then toilets were flushed, faces were washed, sometimes here and there a comb ran through hair and a brush ran on teeth, and then there was the breakfast tray and after that the voice of the nurse that loudly reported on the state of the tables. And now it was Mrs Nasseri's voice that filled the rooms and the ward, and the doctors came one by one to see their patients, and then the ward doctor who examined outside patients. Vaji was standing by the window in the room. The bandage-face had been taken to the operating room and Nahid was drinking tea from her flask at the door of her former room.

'Is Mrs Vajiheh Vassel, bed number twenty-two here?'

At hearing these words, Vaji felt goose pimples. She turned. It was a young pretty woman in a white dress with a file in her hand, a smile at the corner of her lips and bright, honey-coloured eyes that were waiting for an answer. Vaji, who had never seen the woman before, went towards her bed. She was walking in a crouch, as though it reduced her pain.

'It's me.'

The smile obviously froze on the woman's face.

'I'm a counsellor. I just wanted to have a few words with you, if it's all right.'

And now the woman was bringing a chair to sit next to Vaji's bed.

'What's the number of your husband's card?'

'2081.'

The woman looked at the file and read out: 'Place of work: Rey. Place of residence: Shahr-e Rey. You're thirty-five. You've got two kids. Daughter, seventeen, son, two. Fifteen years' difference is rather a lot, isn't it?'

'I couldn't have kids. I was undergoing treatment until God gave Reza to me.'

'Who's he staying with now?'

'With my daughter Farrokh. When Farrokh goes to school, my mother takes care of him.'

'It's two months that you've been hospitalised here. Okay, the Rey Hospital has introduced you. Dr Farsi. Well, excuse me for asking; do you have any problems with your daughter?'

'No.'

'Look, Mrs Vassel, I'm a counsellor. I call on most of the patients. My job is not to interfere with the private affairs of anyone. But I have to solve problems as far as I can. I mean, I like to do so and my job requires me to do so as well. You know, for instance, if you're hospitalised and there's noone to take care of your child, we could introduce him to a kindergarten, or stuff like that. Okay, so you don't have any problems with your daughter. Would you like to use the kindergarten?'

'No, my mother's there.'

'About your husband – his work place, salary, his behaviour. I ask, does he treat you and the kids well?'

'Yes, only he doesn't bring Reza here.'

The woman took notes with her small white hands.

'I'll talk to your husband. Now, about the hospital – for instance your roommates, the nurses, the doctors – is the food good? Do you have any complaints?'

'Noone bothers me.'

'You mean you're ignored?'

'No, it's all the same to me. The food is always there, others are there too. They don't annoy me.'

'Okay, so there's no problem in this regard. If you have a problem or question about anything in particular, I'm all ears.'

The woman didn't expect Vaji to say anything. But just to have said something, Vaji said, 'This Mr Azarmi talks too much. Always talking on the phone.'

The woman looked at the files.

'He talks too much. He's got no other care in the world.'

'If you were in his shoes – twenty years old, in love with a schoolgirl, left leg crippled, left eye blinded and the right one to lose sight soon. With a body full of mortar shell fragments that can't be removed. You only see his laughs and his outside.'

'But he says his eye will get well.'

'I've talked to him. He's getting wind of his condition only little by little. Nevertheless I'll ask the head nurse to change your room so that his phone calls won't bother you.'

'No, no, it's okay here. If I later wanted to …'

'As you wish. Any questions?'

'About my illness. When can I go home?'

'Doctor said you have a small cyst in your stomach and intestine that will gradually diminish with the use of drugs, but you shouldn't hurry. You've got to be patient. According to the doctor who's treating you, you'll definitely get well. The only problem is that the progress is very slow and gradual. You've got to bear it so that you'll be cured a hundred percent.'

'Doctor said the same.'

'Yes, there's nothing more to it. Any other problems?'

'No, Thanks a lot.'

'If you need to see me, call extension 208, or come to my room on the first floor, number 109.'

Vaji followed her to the door and then saw her waiting at the elevator. So she doesn't call on all the patients. She only goes to some of them. Yesterday Mr Azarmi, and now Vaji.

She tried to get up but she couldn't. With every movement, the mild pain in her belly climaxed and shot through her bone marrow. The phone had rung and now a woman's voice resonated in the corridor. 'Bed number six, telephone; bed number six, telephone.'

The woman with the bandaged face was carried in on a movable bed. A man in a green uniform went to the top of the patient's bed and stood there, and another man, fat and robust, stared at Vaji's face: 'Sister, turn your face around.'

Vaji turned her face to the wall. She had already seen how two men lifted the patient and dropped her on the bed with all their might. She could still remember the pain of that moment. Having opened her eyes, for a moment she had seen over her the man's round and fleshy face with that green cap, pushing her bed to and fro. They had lifted her just like a leg of mutton and thrown her onto the bed so that the man waiting over the bed would grab the corner of the sheet and drag it onto the bed and then jump down in a quick leap and then the nurse would come with a white gown to cover the patient. Although the bandage-face was dressed, the nurse would still come to put her gown in order and pull the sheet smooth and then connect the serum to her arm and hang the urine bag from the bed, and then it would be over. The surgery was over and now Nahid was standing by the patient, looking down at her.

'Cheekiness is written all over her face. These Tehranis can only think of their appearance: "Ah, how big my nose is! How ugly I am with this nose! How about having a nose job?"'

Vaji said under her breath indifferently, 'She's had an accident.'

'It's an excuse, just an excuse. Why do you believe her? I know these Tehranis well. The accident is just an excuse for her.'

Vaji closed her eyes. She was in no mood for Nahid's words. But Nahid left the room without a word. Azarmi's voice could be heard:

'You go there every day? In this hot weather? You'll get tired. No, who am I to say I don't want you to? You did a good thing to enroll in those repeat examination classes. No, I swear, it's not for my sake. I'm sure you won't come to see me when you leave home. Well, yes, friends and relatives may say you failed because of me. For example, your classmates may say her love went to the war, got crippled and she failed the exam. I'm not joking. Then they'd sing, "Happy wedding, but watch out for the wrecked leg …" Oh, come on, why are you crying? I was just kidding. Ashraf, you just don't know how sad I am. I don't care about anything in the world. Come on and see me for a bit. Don't come to my room if you don't want to. It's all right in the garden. Oh, really? Congratulations? Your sister gave birth to what? Twins? How wonderful! How many kids do *you* want …?'

Vaji thought that this man would never be short of breath. But queerly, Azarmi's voice didn't bother her any more. She could see that there, outside her room, life was still going on. She could see the corridor through the door. The old Arab man was walking slowly with the IV stand in his hand. His gown was open from top to bottom in the back, and he had crumpled the two sides of the gown from behind in his hands. He slowly pushed the IV stand forward and walked. His black, crumpled buttocks showed from the back. He walked to the elevator and then slowly pulled the IV stand back and returned. Now he had a white scarf on his head. He saw Vaji from the corridor. He nodded to her. Vaji smiled and the man started walking again. Wheelchairs were coming and going. A man with a leg that was no more, or an arm that was no more, or an eye that was no more. Pain filled Vaji's belly. She closed her eyes. She clawed at her belly with all her strength. A cold sweat drenched her body; she had goose pimples. She tried to think of Reza and of Farrokh and Mokhtar, but the pain wouldn't let go of her until the moment of numbness.

When she opened her eyes, Farrokh was looking over her.

'Mom, are you feeling better?'

'Yes my daughter.'

'When will you come home?'

'Very soon. How was your exam?'

And Farrokh had smiled, with that calm smile and those teeth that were in a straight line and caught the eye in the black frame of the *chador*. And her smile was becoming fainter and fainter, so much so that it wasn't there any more, and now Farrokh had gone far away and the pain didn't crawl up the legs any more; rather, it was always there, inside that large egg that didn't resemble an egg at all.

After a few hours, the pain started, not from the legs but from the belly, and it soared, stretched, reached the head, and from the other side dragged itself down to the knee. Then the body was hot and the pain contracted. Then it curled itself up and panted there inside that egg, and then the large drops of sweat froze on the body and then came the moment when Vaji would release herself free and relieved on the sweat-drenched pillow.

In the morning Nahid had come over Vaji's bed with her bag in hand, had kissed her and left after saying goodbye. Vaji looked around. The bandage-face wasn't there either. She had left too. Without saying goodbye. Yesterday or the day before? She couldn't remember. How many of them now? Six, seven, eight, nine. The ninth one was also gone. The first one was Mrs Amini, who had cancer. She was a nurse herself; how had she failed to realise? She would walk in the corridor without a care. She would put her hand on her left breast and press it. She had a secret there that she had kept to herself. Vaji had stayed with her in one room for a week. She had not even guessed. She had said that there was a pain in her heart, and then one morning she wasn't there any more. They said she had had cancer. One word: cancer. And she had put her hand on that secret every day, every hour and every moment, pressing it lest it would spill out, and now the ninth one was also gone. Vaji thought, one day it will be my turn to get up and kiss my roommates and tell them that I'm dismissed too. Goodbye. I don't have cancer. I know it. I would know if I had it. It can't be as ridiculous as that. Mrs Amini was a nurse, she had told Vaji herself. How had she failed to realise? How had she failed to cut that secret out and throw it out? And she put her hand so firmly on her left breast everyday and stroked it, as if it were her kid. As if it were her husband and she had to live with him day and night and stroke his head. Vaji thought that it was closer to you than your kid, your husband, than everything. It was essentially yourself. The secret you must conceal and stroke, and there's nowhere you can put it so that it won't return. Because it will come back and settle there on your left breast. And when you raise your hand to pull it out from the roots, you'll stroke it again inadvertently, as if stroking your kid, as if stroking your husband – no, even closer than them – as if it were yourself. 'What's with you over there?'

Vaji looked at the bulging stomach of the woman sitting on the bandage-face's bed. She had lost the count of patients who came and left. The woman was sweetening her tea.

'Nothing's wrong with me. I mean, I know what my problem is, but I can't mention it.'

The woman had not understood.

'A small tumour. It'll be cured with medicine.'

'I'm seven months' pregnant. Doctor says the baby's died in my womb. I don't believe it. How is it possible that something dies inside you and you don't realise it? Tomorrow they'll operate on me. Do you think the operation will hurt?

'Not much.'

'You want tea?'

'No.'

And when the woman fell silent, the familiar and quiet voice of Azarmi could be heard:

'Why not? Every time I look in the mirror I'm ashamed of myself. What have you done? You're right not to come here. You would barely answer my greetings when I was healthy and lively. With this situation it's obvious. And when I soon lose my eye, you'll be supposed to hold my hand. I'm not talking nonsense. Doctor said it himself. If I go abroad after a lot of formalities and spend a lot of money, they just might be able to save my other eye, but only "just might" … For your mother's sake, please don't cry. I couldn't make myself tell you. It's a week that my heart's bleeding, but I saw that it's not fair. I didn't go there to have fun. I went for the sake of God and the Prophet. I know that I'm being tested. But then what's your fault? No, Ashraf, I swear, I'm not joking. For God's sake don't cry. I fell in love with you one day, and now I kiss your lovely face and tell you, we have different paths to follow. Forget about me. Just suppose that I went to pieces there. Over. As for your letters – either have your mother come over and collect them, or I'll burn the lot myself. For God's sake don't cry. You'll cry for a day, a week, a month; then you'll forget it all. But I won't be able to take it if I'm before your eyes every day. Nothing's happened yet. God's testing me. The more I think about it, the more I see that our paths are different. I swear on your life and Hassan's, I won't forgive you if you hurt yourself. Don't sob like that. Don't tear my heart apart, don't make me more ruined than I am. Don't mention it. Good luck. Goodbye.'

And he had burst into tears. Vaji curled up her entire body and pushed herself forward to try and see through the door Azarmi going, but she couldn't. Two nurses were sitting quietly at the desk with their backs to Azarmi. Now again the pain was wringing Vaji's stomach and then filling her entire body. She closed her eyes from the pain. She bit her lip. She opened her eyes for a moment. Her roommate was ringing the emergency bell. Vaji shoved her fist against her belly. She knew that painkillers were no use any more. She passed out from the intensity of the pain. When she came to, Farrokh's hand was on her forehead. 'Mom, I love you. How are you? Can you hear me?'

Vaji smiled. She smiled at that face and those transparent, framed eyes. Mokhtar was standing a little farther from her.

Vaji said under her breath, 'How many more days should I stay here?'

Mokhtar's upper lip twanged. His face went white. He said quietly, 'Bear it a few more days. Then we'll go home.'

Vaji tried to say, 'Come here,' but she was short of breath. And Mokhtar came to her. Without hearing anything, from the woman's lips that were moving, he had realised that he should go close to hear her words.

'You remember Mr Azarmi? The man next door. Go to him.'

And Mokhtar was about to leave when Vaji's lips had moved again and she had said, 'Take Farrokh as well. Take Farrokh as well. Azarmi's a nice guy. Don't leave him alone.'

FERESHTEH SARI

The Lost Time

It was a strange hour of the day. Three o'clock. Since her childhood, she had not been able to help being tempted at this nostalgic time of the day. Sunset always had a feeling of the past, and dusk was the doorway to the past. Noontime was like future, and morning was the threshold of future. Midday looked like present. But she didn't know what to do with this hour that had passed the future, without reaching the threshold of the past; she didn't know what to do with this suspended time.

An insidious wind was blowing. She did up her last button. A dry draught was running over her body through the end of her sleeve. She accelerated her steps to warm up a little. On the street, heads ducked in collars were passing rapidly. Then the street became empty. Noone could be seen, there was only the anxiety of awaiting someone entering the scene.

She stopped by the deserted street. A car was approaching her. She called out her destination aloud. A half-brake and the sound of rubber screeching on asphalt. She called out her destination to any car that did or didn't slow down.

Suddenly she was astonished at hearing the word coming out of her mouth. She felt that she had uttered a meaningless word. Finally, without saying anything, she waved at a car.

She sank in the rear seat. The mild warmth inside the car gave her a feeling of languor. She looked at the streets from behind the window. She could see the cold through the undulating branches of the trees in the wind. A few times it seemed to her that a head stuck out from behind a tree and directly looked at her and made faces at her.

The car got away from familiar streets and turned into a one-way street, on the two sides of which there were houses with moss-covered walls and shadowy curtains. She could see the silence and hear the sad sound of oldness. She turned to the driver and asked, 'Why are you going this way?'

It seemed to her that in the front seat only two hands were turning the steering wheel, and that the space above the hands turned to her. It was as if someone had turned towards her with the question 'What?' and she realised that she didn't have a voice of her own. For a few moments, she closed her eyes and told herself, 'I'm not feeling well; that's all. I'll be there shortly.'

Then with the terror of a child who has let go of her mother's hand in a crowd and is just beginning to realise that she is lost, she said 'Where to?'

All around her was full of legs. She was making her way through the fence of the jumble of legs, and she could still see only legs. Her head was no higher than the legs' knees. First she had burst out laughing and simultaneously, on realising that she was lost, a silent cry had swirled in her heart. It was as if a cold storm was blowing in her soul, as if the end of a cone had been put in her mouth and filled with a cold wind. She had pushed the legs aside with the back of her little hands, and her laughter had turned into sobs, and she had seen that the mass of intertwined fences of legs were only four people that had come between her mother and her when she got lost.

Behind the mist-covered window, her tears framed the faces of women, and broke them. None of them looked like her mother. 'Mom!' got fragmented with the hiccupping of her cry. Someone stepped on her foot. Her cry became more heart-wrenching. A cracking sound was heard and her pink shell crumbled. The button of her dress fell off. When she removed the button, she didn't think that the cotton inside the soft doll might fall out and the doll would go flat. The button stood for the doll's navel. The cloth was creased and tied to the navel button under its stomach. The white cotton spurted out. She put her hand on her stomach and started waiting in horror for the cotton to spurt out of her own stomach. She was screaming with a choked voice, running to left and right. There were strange things in the shops. She stood at the fabric shop. Maybe her mother would make another doll for her from the waste cloth that she bought, and then she wouldn't remove its navel button again. She ran to another shop window in agitation. She was squeezing her stomach with her hands but she felt that the cotton was falling out and her stomach was getting emptier and her feet softer. She had cried all winter. Mother said, 'Let me sew it.' She said, 'No, she's dead now, didn't you hear her scream?'

'What's the matter? Why are you pressing on your belly? You have stomach ache? I just went into the shop to ask about that fabric's price. What's become of you?'

The car turned into a half-dark street, a winding alley that kept getting narrow and then wide again, and along every bend it seemed as if the car was entrapped between the tilting walls. She closed her eyes, but the spiralling movement was such that she felt as if she was passing through the winding intestine of an animal. The tall, oblique walls of the street were covered with moss. Along a bend she saw a house with a very tall wooden door.

She couldn't remember why she had come out of the house. Perhaps she had wanted to buy something? She felt that she had got too far away. But from what? She didn't know. Perhaps she had made a gesture with her hand, and that was why the car had stopped before that tall wooden door, which looked like the gate of a town. She held out to the driver the banknote she had had in her hand since she got in the car. She couldn't tell if she was walking towards the wooden door with short steps or it was the door that was moving towards her. She turned and saw no trace of the car. The street was too narrow for the car to have passed through so quickly. Had she ridden in a car at all, or was it a hand that had put her on that narrow curve in front of the curves engraved on the rotten wood?

She shook her head, as if repelling a disturbing thought from her like an obstinate housefly. She pushed the door and found it very light. It was as if she had pushed aside a curtain with her shoulder. As soon as she passed through the half-open door, the memory of the house settled into her mind.

The transparent dimness of the space is labyrinthine. Having pushed aside each curtain, another curtain falls down. In search of the depth of transparent water in concentric circles, the sight becomes dim. Frames of blackened silver cover the walls. She looks at a framed mirror. A huge crowd gathers. She is dazzled by the resemblance of all of them to her. Once a woman takes a candle from the candlestick, all take candles in hand. She goes out of the ring of candleholders and she becomes a single person again.

She passes through a vestibule. On her right there is a sterile palm tree from which an old man with a white beard has been hanged. A naked child is sitting beneath the old man's feet. A dry wind shakes the stationary image and a coin drops out of the hanged man onto the ground at the base of the tree. The child picks up the coin and glances at a female slave whom noone is willing to purchase. Her eyes, as if framed by rings of permanent mascara, are shining; but the slave is not young any more. On her left, an old mule is auctioned by the blows of a stick, its black and innocent eyes get full and then empty of tears. The mule doesn't get sold. It is skinned right there and its meat is put to auction. The slave stays staring at the base of the palm tree. The naked child gets up – or the slave's affectionate glance lifts her up and takes her towards her owner. She puts the gold coin in the palm of the man's hand and takes the slave's hand. The slave hugs the child and goes away behind a ruin. The child is sticking to the slave's neck so hard it's as if she is scared to lose her eternal mother again. The moaning of a cat. The throwing of the cat's head from behind the ruin, and a moment later, smoke that smells of cooked cat's head.

A fortuneteller in black veil is sitting at a spread on which lies a handful of chickpeas in a queer formation. Beside her, the judge reads out a sentence, and a convict is taken towards the palm tree whose fruit is an old man. The judge stands by the spread of a peddler, who has laid yellow agates and milky coloured beads in the middle of a rosary made from palm date stones. The judge has turned his back to the execution of the sentence he has issued. Away from the square, an old woman who collects thorn roots pays no attention to anything but the thorn winds of the desert. A few pieces of damp plaster fall off the swelling of the parlour and half of the old woman runs after thorn winds. Behind the desert is a garden covered with short, button-like mushrooms. From among the mushrooms, creeping reptiles are peering. On the rotten leaves under the plane trees, hives of mildews can be seen. From a sack of rice on the trunk of a pistachio tree – whose burnt pistachios are smiling – salty water trickles drop by drop. The sound of the drops is the only sound in the world. Thousands of dead magpies are stuck to the ancient trees like blackened fruits. She feels that she must walk on the hive of mildew to hear another sound. She leans against a green cypress and closes her eyes for a moment. White cotton covers everywhere. Feeling a cold wind, she opens her eyes. The huge wooden door is so heavy it cannot be moved. She is panting. With painstaking effort she opens the door as wide as her shoulder width. She comes out of the narrow and wide curves of the spiralling street. It strikes her that the car she had got off from has passed across the bend of the street. The street has a forlorn look. The buildings are of an architectural style she has never seen before. Perhaps when she was in the car she didn't look to see how far she had gone. For a while she looks round in confusion, and finally chooses the direction that seems to her to be heading downward.

She waves at several cars, but none of them stop. Perhaps another gesture is required, a gesture she doesn't know of. A car stops and a passenger gets off. Without hesitation, she gets in: 'Hafez Avenue.'

She is impatiently waiting to see her familiar streets. She must have come too far. But the appearance of the city becomes stranger as the car moves down. None of the shops, signs or the architecture of the houses look familiar. She notices a square surrounding the intertwined circles of other squares. The car stops on the first ring. She wants to say something, but the driver opens the door for her and waits for the fare. She opens her bag and takes out a banknote. The driver looks at her as at a lunatic. And with a strange accent she hardly understands, he says, 'But this belongs to the Middle Ages.'

The car goes away. She stands there and sees the car reach the common centre of the circles and go out along a small radius.

Fariba Vafi

My Mother Behind the Glass

I told Sister Ashraf: 'I'm going home to fetch my books.' I was lying to her. If I told her that I wanted to go and take mom's picture out of the album, she wouldn't let me go. She would make faces at me and say something rude. Because my mom is her stepmother. And ever since mom's been thrown in there she hates her guts. Still she doesn't know what's happened to mom. But then, how do you expect her to know? You should go there and see for yourself to believe. When they caught mom, Ashraf came home, grabbed my hand and took me to their home. She wouldn't say anything. I said:

'What about my mom?'

Like when she pitied me, she narrowed her eyes. 'You're a grownup girl now, you don't need your mom.'

Then her husband came and Ashraf didn't say anything any more. I hated her husband so much. He looked at you in a way you got to get ashamed of yourself … Actually if it were not for the sake of those two little hellraisers of Sister Ashraf – Majid and Mahin – I would never have stayed there. Although, if I didn't stay there I'd have nowhere else to go. My brother Reza had gone to Tehran. I say that whatever happened had something to do with that woman. I don't know how she had broken it to Reza but he just saw red.

That day brother wasn't speaking at all, but he had blushed. His wife was holding her head up high and looked at you in such a way that made you sick. Mom had shrunken in a corner and peeped out at Reza furtively. Sister Ashraf kept wriggling around brother Reza, begging of him not to go. But brother's look, with those bloodshot eyes, was horrible. In the end he said, 'Get out of my way!'

To be honest, I was afraid of brother Reza too, and in my heart, I wished he'd leave so that we could be at peace. You know, he pestered mom so much. Every time I came back from school, I saw them quarrelling over something. And brother Reza always took sides with his wife. If her own mom were alive, he wouldn't have let his wife be free to be so cheeky. Brother didn't look at mom at all when he was leaving. They packed up all their belongings and left. Ashraf left after them. It was only then that I understood how awful it all was. The house became somehow different. It sickened your heart. Mom held her head up and said, 'To hell with them! Let them go.'

Then she got up and tidied the house. She was pretending not to be bothered, but she was upset. I knew it. I got up and went into the yard. When I came back, I saw that mom's eyes were red. Mom always cried furtively, as if she was ashamed of someone seeing her tears. But I did see her tears. And from behind that damn windowpane. Yes, there … When I looked up, I saw that mom's face was covered with tears and the hollows under her eyes were full of wrinkles. When mom wanted to go out, for an hour – oh, for a full hour – she would sit in front of the mirror and rub the skin on her face. As if she wanted to go to a wedding. Sometimes she would put cucumber slices on her face. It made me laugh to look at her. When she had finished with her skin, she'd start tampering with her eyes and eyebrows. Mom's got very big eyes. And they're always misty somehow. And she's got long eyelashes. When she put eyeliner on her eyes she became so pretty. Then she would take the tweezers out and start fighting the hair on her face. Then she'd put red lipstick on her lips. Then she'd look at herself in the mirror and smile. Then she'd change her dress and put on a very fragrant perfume. I would also rush forward, and she'd put a little perfume on my dress too. Then she'd get up and leave.

Mom took very good care of herself since Aqa had died. She went to parties very often. It was as if it was retaliation for those days when Aqa wouldn't let her go anywhere. When Aqa was alive, mom didn't have the right to go anywhere. I don't know why. But once Aqa had seen mom chatting and giggling with Yousef Aqa the haberdasher. I still remember what Aqa did to mom that day. He undid his belt and beat the sunlight out of mom. As mom was being beaten up she cried, 'Leave me alone, you rotten heap of bones.'

Because Aqa was very old. That's why when mom called him 'rotten heap of bones' or 'old hyena', she would get Aqa's goat and he would beat her up more. Then Aqa got ill and died. Oh God, what awful days they were. Mom was crying like everyone else, but I knew that she wasn't grieving that much. You know, she'd never loved Aqa. She would always say that herself. Mom always used to curse her parents because they had ruined her life, but I knew that she wasn't cursing them from the bottom of her heart, for I'd seen that she secretly took many things for them from home: rice, ghee oil and stuff like that. And on the New Year's Eve she gave them money so that they'd buy me gifts or send her presents on their behalf. I had realised all this.

And once, Aqa's older wife caught mom red-handed and made an awful scandal out of it. Then they swore at each other and pulled each other's hair and had a big fight. Aqa's wife and my mom used to fight very frequently. Then Aqa's wife got cancer and died. Mom thought that everything would change and Aqa would quit picking on her and stop beating her up, but Aqa's temper became worse. He'd always want to know with whom mom was coming and going. Since Aqa's wife was dead, Reza and Ashraf ignored mom. And then Aqa would beat mom up over the most trivial things. Mom used to say, 'I'll kill myself someday and get rid of this damn life.'

And once, she was about to do something serious. That day she had received an awful lot of beating from Aqa. She made as big a noise as she could, repeatedly swearing that she would kill herself. That night she took out two tubes of pills from the closet and was about to swallow them when I rolled in my bed and said under my breath, 'Mom.'

I pretended that I was calling her in my sleep. Mom's eyes fell on me for a moment. That is, my eyes were closed, but I knew that she was looking at me. Then she suddenly hugged me and burst into tears. I was in mom's arms and my hair had become quite wet with her tears. I wished Aqa were not so bad-tempered. I wished to always sleep in my mom's arms. I wish I had remained little like that, so that mom wouldn't always leave me at home and go out … Oh God, I wish mom was home now and I hadn't come to Ashraf's house. I wish she'd taken me in there with her. What would have been wrong with that?

Once when she was going out, I told her, 'Mom, take me with you.'

'You sit and do your homework. I'm going out and will be back soon.'

She always said she'd be back soon and she never was. I secretly followed her into the alley. I saw her covering her face with the *chador*, quickly going into the street and getting into a cherry-coloured Paykan car. The driver was a young man wearing a scarlet shirt, and with his eyes he looked at mom in a peculiar way. I didn't like him at all. Then the Paykan took off and left. I returned home alone. When mom came back, she had bought me a beautiful hairclip. I said, 'I don't want it.'

I was full of grudges. I was sulking. But mom was in high spirits. She took the hair clip and fitted it to her own hair. She had dyed her hair lately. Blonde. It suited her so much. She seemed to be getting younger and younger. She stood before the mirror and smiled. It was as though someone else was looking at her from the mirror. Perhaps it was the same young man. I had never seen mom so happy before. But I didn't want to talk to her, I don't know why. There was something wrong with mom's smiles. I didn't like them at all. If you want my idea, it was all that young man's fault that they got mom.

I went to the cellar in Ashraf's house. I sat there and wept. I missed my mom so much. Once when Ashraf came into the cellar, I quickly wiped my tears. But she seemed to have noticed them. 'What's wrong?'

'Nothing.'

Then she sat beside me. 'Perhaps you're missing her?'

I didn't say anything, and just looked down. Tears fell of their own accord. Sister Ashraf ran her hand through my hair, 'You shouldn't miss her. If she had had a tiny bit of emotion in her, she wouldn't have left you and gone out with strangers. She's caused disgrace for all of us.'

My tears kept running down my face. Sister Ashraf seemed to take pity on me. 'Okay, I'll take you to see her. Don't cry so much.'

Then she took me there and told me that she would wait by the door and not come inside, because her husband would skin her alive if he got wind of it. Then she said, 'I wish she'd learn her lesson; I wish she'd come to her senses and not do such things any more.'

That day I went in and sat behind that glass. Sister Ashraf stayed outside and didn't come inside with me. I was scared, I was terribly scared. It was too crowded. My heart was beating like mad. Then suddenly there were sounds on the other side. Then a woman came behind the glass. I say a woman, because at first I didn't recognise mom, but it was her all right. It was mom. How she had changed. Her face was covered with wrinkles and her eyes had receded into the sockets. She had become an old, old woman. I pitied her so much. I burst into tears. 'Mom.'

Mom's face was covered with tears. She had an old *chador* on her head and she was sitting behind that thick glass like a stranger and just kept on weeping. I told her, 'Mom, please do something so that they'll let you out. I don't want to go to Ashraf's house any more.'

Mom kept weeping behind the glass.

NOUSHIN SALARI

Like a Well

When she picked up the phone, there was silence at the other end of the line. Jumbled sounds were heard as if from far away, from far, far away.

But shortly there was the sound of a beep and then laughter.

'Hello!'

Who was it that said 'hello' like that?

Javad asked, 'Who is it?' He was standing in the doorway of the bedroom.

Thank God the kid hadn't woken up. Who was it that laughed so familiarly from a long way off?

It was someone who said 'hello' and dragged on the letter *L*, someone who dragged ...

'Shahrzad?'

Javad said, 'Shahrzad?' and shook his head. He didn't know her.

And it was as if Shahrzad was there. She said, 'Hello!' and dragged on the letter *L*. She used to sit beside her on the bench in the classroom, in the second or third grade. And now she was laughing.

When she said first 'hello' there was a pause, and after the pause the voice came again:

'Hello!'

Whose voice was this?

Shahrzad asked, 'How are you?'

And she was still thinking of that 'hello'.

Shahrzad said, 'I got your number by chance.'

She asked, 'By chance?'

Shahrzad said, 'Yes, I ran into your cousin on the street. She's been here but I didn't know.' And she asked, 'Why didn't you write to me?'

'Because letters …' What do people tell each other in such circumstances? 'I was too busy.'

Shahrzad said, 'How's Javad?'

And she looked at the door that was empty now. Javad must have gone to bed. 'Javad's fine.'

Shahrzad asked, 'The kid looks like which of you?' Shahrzad had left before she married Javad.

And she laughed. Now, after a pause, someone was laughing. She said, 'She looks like a kid.'

'What do you look like now? Like the same picture that …' She meant the wedding picture. The only picture she had sent her. How long before was it?

She asked, 'What time is it over there?' And she didn't know why she had asked this. Perhaps in dead of night no question had any relevance to its answer.

Shahrzad said, 'It's five in the morning. What about there?'

'It's early evening.'

'So you were asleep?'

How could one tell someone so far away that one had been tossing and turning in bed?

'Have you got any news from the kids?'

The kids? What kids? She didn't ask. Shahrzad herself said, 'The kids from school.'

A metal globe was revolving in the classroom; all the blue stains, all the green stains and all the brown stains were revolving.

'I sometimes see some of them.' And when was that sometimes? When she was standing at the end of a queue and she stuck out her head to see how long the queue was, and a familiar face caught her eye; in the office of the pediatrician, or when she was with Javad waiting for a taxi on the street, and a face smiled behind the window of a car?

Shahrzad said, 'What was that girl's name?'

'Which one?'

'The one who sang for us one day and all of us cried for no reason.' Shahrzad was laughing.

And she didn't know, she didn't know anything. She could remember a black-eyed girl singing, 'My eyes are your home, your home.' Where is she now and what is she doing? Perhaps she had her own Javad; and perhaps she was calling someone too.

A metal globe …

Shahrzad said, 'I thought I'd lost you forever.' Shahrzad had now tilted her head and was drawing lines on a corner of a sheet of paper. Just as she used to tilt her head in the classroom and draw intertwined lozenges on a corner of a sheet of paper; a tiny beehive, so tiny that only a single bee could jump from one lozenge to another inside it.

Silence was full of jumbled sounds. She said, 'We moved houses and I …'

Why didn't anyone invent a new language? So many people were far from one another and noone invented a new language so that a cough would have a meaning, and the dragging of words and even this silence. She said, 'I didn't have time.'

Shahrzad said, 'I'll finish my studies this year.' And she laughed. 'I have lost count of the babies I have delivered.' She had totally forgotten that Shahrzad was studying midwifery.

'Isn't it over yet?' Javad was now standing in the doorway again looking at her.

Shahrzad said, 'I can't stay here any more. I must find a place to go to.'

She asked, 'Where?'

Javad shrugged and left.

Shahrzad said, 'I must find a place.'

And again there was silence and jumbled sounds, and a woman sounded to say 'Hello!' somewhere very, very far away.

Shahrzad asked, 'Do you remember that literature teacher of ours?' and she looked at the empty doorway again.

'Which one?'

'The one who used to say, kids, the worst thing in the world is that you don't have anywhere to go.'

Voices were intermingling somewhere far away, very far away, and that woman – what had become of that woman?

A metal globe that …

And perhaps Shahrzad was still drawing lozenges and lozenges and that beehive was growing bigger.

Shahrzad said, 'That teacher was right.' And then said that she had to go. Because the owner of the telephone would be back any moment.

The silence was once again full of voices that came from somewhere far away, very far away. And then Shahrzad was saying her goodbyes, and next she asked, 'Do you remember?'

And she just said, 'I remember.' And before the click of the phone, after a pause, there was a voice: 'You remember.' The voice had hit somewhere and echoed. It was her own voice that echoed. Like when you stand before a high mountain and you say, 'I remember,' and the voice echoes, she remembers.

A metal globe that rotated round itself. A girl who sang, a teacher who wiped chalk dust from his fingers, a man who constantly stood in doorways and shook his head, and all the empty beehives …

She passed through the doorway and sat on the edge of the bed.

Javad was lying with his face to the wall. He asked, 'Finished?'

She didn't say anything. She was accustomed to it.

A metal globe that rotated …

That voice was her own voice and was echoing. She stretched her legs one at a time. She lay on her back. The voice was her own voice. Not like a mountain. It was like a well, a well into which you stuck your head and shouted a secret. And then, when the bamboo canes of the well became flutes, they would play that secret. She clasped her hands on her swollen belly and closed her eyelids. Just like a well … And tomorrow, would any flute play beside any beehive?

ROYA SHAPOURIAN

Dahlia

When I entered the hall with a watermelon under my arm, I looked
ridiculous. It was heavy – 8 kilos and 250 grams. We had gone to
Tajrish Bridge for a walk when Hamid had longed for a watermelon.
He said, 'The season will soon be over.' And he did his best to
pick two ripe watermelons – the kind with a white patch grown on
them.

I said, 'If mother was here she would pick a watermelon that
would make the shopkeeper's jaw drop.'

He frowned.

I said, 'Come on, let's take one for her.'

He said, 'Only on the condition that you don't go in. I'll give it
to the doorman to take it to her.'

I said, 'Forget it.'

To change the subject, he said, 'Iron my shirts tomorrow. I have
so many meetings this week.'

I said, 'I'll call on mother tomorrow. I've got so many things to
do for you that I can't find the time to call on her.'

I stood at the doorway for a moment and looked at her. She was sitting on her bed. She was bending over, clipping her toenails with trembling hands. It seemed that she was whispering something. At home, when she wiped the tables and chairs with a dusting cloth, she sang Delkash's songs, but her voice was more delicate.

She used to say, 'The times have made my voice week.' And she laughed until she started coughing.

I went forward. I put the watermelon on the bedside table and said:

'Hello, mother!' And I kissed her cheek.

She said, 'Hello, my sweetheart.'

I said, 'How are you?'

She said, 'Not bad. How's Saeed's mumps? Is he better?'

I said, 'Yes, and it's not contagious any more. He gave me hell all this time. I'd got him out of Sara's room. All the time I was careful not to let her catch it from him.'

She took in a deep breath and shook her head. Then she bent over again to clip her little toenail.

Hamid said, 'We don't have enough room for ourselves. And you keep saying, "My mother, my mother!" Can't you see that this is a flat? The kids will grow soon and they'll need rooms of their own. You think I like it? I wish to God I had a garden with a huge palace in the middle, with long corridors lined with rooms. I'd give one to Mamma. But like this, it's better both for us and for that poor thing. God bless her.'

'Did you say *God*? So manly of you. You can only tell fairy tales. A large corridor ...'

It was a pity that tears choked me; otherwise I would have said more. Hamid didn't know that I had been used to waking up with the sound of mother's coughing. For years on end, she woke up at the crack of dawn, tidied up the house and kept coughing. When she stood in the kitchen to prepare breakfast, the coughing wouldn't give her a respite. No matter how many times I said, 'Mother, go sit and take a rest to calm down,' she wouldn't listen. She was accustomed to work. The dust, the broom, the coldness of the kitchen – I don't know what made her cough so hard. She used to refuse to take her pills. But now she took them regularly. That's why she had become so weak and wouldn't speak. Only a trace of memories remains on her face, by which you can recognise her.

Mother pointed at my belly and said, 'No more in the pipeline?'

I said, 'No. I'd even sent Sara to kindergarten to have more time for my own things. But she wouldn't stay there.'

Mother smiled a pale smile and didn't say anything.

I told Hamid, 'It's natural for kids to nag. You just shouldn't listen to him. The first two or three days are always difficult.'

He said, 'But I'd die for my kids.'

I said, 'A man shouldn't be so emotional.'

Finally, on the fourth or fifth day, when Hamid came in through the door, Sara ran to him and said, 'Dad, do you love me? True to God, do you love me?'

Hamid stood dazed in the doorway and said, 'Yes, dear, I love you so much.'

Sara said, 'So don't send me to kindergarten.'

And Hamid immediately accepted.

I said, 'Shouldn't you have asked my opinion too? You mustn't spoil the child like that. I'll go and enroll her in the kindergarten again.'

Mother said, 'Thanks so much for the watermelon.'

I said, 'You're an expert. Go ahead, tap it and see if it sounds good.' But I thought, 'What's the use? What if it turned out to be white?' You couldn't trust Hamid's choice.

Mother always used to say, 'Life is like buying a watermelon; everyone thinks he can pick a good one for himself, but many people are fooled all the same. You've got to be a real expert.'

And it seems as if you won't find out until you break it open, and taste it to the very last mouthful. At the other end of the room, an old woman was lying; she kept pressing the bell so that somebody would come to her.

I said, 'Mother, have you made friends with the people around you?'

She said, 'Yes, very much.'

I don't know whether she said it out of rage or indifference. Since she's come here, I can't recognise the expressions of her face properly. It's as if she's extremely far from me and I can't understand her any more. I wish she said something, even blamed me. I know that she only wishes for one thing: not to be here any more. And every time I come here I wish I could say, 'Mother, I've come to take you home.'

I said, 'But you know, mother, the kids like to be up till late at night and watch TV. They make noises. They'll interrupt your sleep. Besides, we have no spare rooms. I'll have to put a cushion for you in the living room. Then, if one day Hamid brings his friends home without any notice ...'

Mother said, 'I've washed the knife. It's in the drawer. Take it and cut the watermelon. And have some.'

I looked around. On the next bed, the same shrunken old woman was lying; she seemed to have become more shrunken than before. Her skin was yellow. Even the whites of her eyes were yellowish. She looked like a piece of crumpled paper thrown in a corner and yellowed by time. I said something to her in the way of a greeting and she started replying in Turkish rapidly. In such instances, the only thing I could say in Turkish was, 'I don't speak Turkish.' Mother couldn't speak more than two or three sentences either, but she understood the language.

Mother said, 'She's in a very bad state. She's so restless.'

On the contrary, mother had sunk into herself so deeply that she hardly moved. Once when I came to visit her, she only opened her mouth to show me that she hadn't put her false teeth in. And she didn't speak to me at all. No matter how many times I said, 'Mother, let me rinse the teeth so that you can put them in,' she turned her back to me and went to sleep. I sat there for a while and looked at her.

Mrs Ebrahimi, the supervisor of the ward, opened the door and called, 'Mrs Taheri, your son's here.'

The old woman on the next bed moved her body on the bed while scratching herself. The son was young, but he had a dishevelled appearance. The back of his blouse was sticking out of his trousers, and his collar was open. As she was coming forward, Mrs Ebrahimi said, 'Sir, it's three weeks since I left a message for you, saying that your mother should be sent to a hospital.'

I said, 'She's got only this one son?'

Mother said, 'No, this is the youngest one. Others have wives and homes. This one also wanted to marry; but then he decided that no woman would live with her in-law, so he brought his mother here. And it seems he's chosen a girl. He's too busy. He seldom comes here.'

She spoke as if she was talking to herself rather than addressing me. A growth of flesh had stuck out of the side of her toenail, and she couldn't remove it, no matter how hard she tried. Her hand was shaking.

I said, 'Let me help you.'

She said 'No,' and pulled back her hand.

The son kissed his mother, and as soon as he sat on the edge of the bed, Mrs Ebrahimi raised her voice. 'Sir, you should pay attention. It's your responsibility to take your mother to hospital. We don't have any responsibility for patients.'

The day we brought mother here, Hamid quickly went through a printed form that said, 'The house has no responsibility for anything.'

I said, 'Mother, here they take good care of you. They look after you. We have our own jobs; we don't have time to take care of you.'

She had looked down; otherwise I would have seen her tears.

Mrs Taheri had raised her head from the pillow and was saying something in Turkish. She spoke so excitedly that I guessed she must be having a row with her son, and that she must be swearing at him. She started loudly and then continued slowly. I guessed that she must be cursing him. Disinherited. The agonies of hell. And she kept scratching her arms and legs as she spoke. The son didn't pay any attention to his mother's words, and as Mrs Taheri raised her voice higher, he tried to answer her calmly.

Mother said, 'I say, next time you come, bring me my embroidery. That pillow cover that I'd sewn in mouse-teeth style, and that small patchwork tablecloth.'

The patchwork was in the form of dahlias, scarlet and lush with petals and sticking out of the background. Mother loved her own name, a name that always reminds me of the Kowkab Khanom[1] in the primary school Persian book, the woman who milked the cows and made yoghurt and cheese.

'Mother, why don't you make yoghurt?'

'Because the shopkeepers must also have their bread and butter; it would ruin their business if I made yoghurt.'

Mother said again, 'I want that white linen with the crochet work I have done on the margins, the one with a butterfly design. I want to have it with me.'

Hamid said, 'The old lady would bring out her bundle and show the flower designs even if a minister plenipotentiary came to see us.'

I said, 'Mother, now that I'm here, please teach me the wheat-flower style; I want to knit a jumper for Saeed. I don't want him to catch cold in winter on the way to school.'

Mother said, 'Get me yarn and I'll knit it myself.'

'No mother, you'll hurt your eyes, you'll get tired out.'

'You no longer recognise my knitting work?'

She always said that. 'Don't you recognise my work? You didn't like the way I washed the dishes?'

Mrs Taheri was saying that Turkish sentence again and Mrs Ebrahimi was arguing with her son. The son said, 'You transfer her and I'll accept all the costs.'

---

1. *Kowkab* in Persian means 'dahlia'.

And as if having run out of patience, standing with her hand on her waist, Mrs Erahimi said, 'We only do our own duties.'

At the other end of the room, an old woman was still ringing the bell.

Mother said, 'Give me my comb from the drawer,' and she undid the elastic band around her hair. She let her hair fall loose around her. It was a mass of white hair without a single black strand in it. She dragged the comb intermittently, and her hand shook among those white locks that coiled around each other. It was as if she was shaking the dust of years from her head. I wished she would look at me and I wished that her look would have the taste of those red and sweet watermelons that she used to cut for us in narrow slices and hand to us when I was a kid. In summer she used to spread a carpet on the terrace and sit, and in the middle of our games, when we were short of breath either from running or from laughing, we would take a slice of watermelon from her hand.

She would say, 'Go for it, go play, don't get beaten by anyone.'

I said, 'Let me plait your hair,' and I took the comb from her hair calmly and ran it through the hair. I wound the end of the lock of hair and started to plait it. My mother turned and smiled at me. On the opposite wall, there was a picture of a weeping willow, with hanging, intertwined branches, either out of fatigue or out of loneliness.

Mrs Ebrahimi and Mrs Taheri's son started to walk away.

It was about time for me to leave too. It was near noon. I would take Saeed from school and go home. When the son was going out of the hall door, his mother dragged herself to the edge of the table and repeated her words. Her breath came out with difficulty and she kept scratching her arms and legs. I wish my mother would also curse me before I left, so that I'd relax a bit. I wished that she shouted at me so bad that I'd get angry and leave.

I said, 'Mother, what's she telling her son?'

Mother smiled and repeated the woman's words: 'A lock of hair on the boy's head is sticking out. She's telling him to run his hand through his hair to smooth it down. She's telling him words of endearment. She is saying, "My dear son wants to become a bridegroom, so he should make himself nice in the mirror, anyone who sees his face will fall in love with him."'

I couldn't take it any more. I got up. In my bag, I had the money for Sara's enrollment. I went to the accounting department and paid the expenses.

The man said, 'Madam, we might not have any vacant places if you return her. Our beds get filled very quickly.'

I said to myself, 'Oh yes, these beds get filled very quickly.' I said, 'No, I won't bring her back. I reassure you.'

No matter what Hamid will say, I'll retort. Because, you know, my mother is so dear to me. I'll see to it that there'll be enough room for everyone. I'll say that the dahlia is a delicate flower; it withers easily. It should be taken care of …

When I was back in the hall, Mrs Taheri was sitting in her bed, stroking her son's head and mother had half-risen to take her pre-midday pills.

I said, 'Mother, pack your things. We're going home.'

QODSI QAZI-NOUR

Eclipse

Nothing is indicative of his footprint, but his presence is everywhere, like heavy air. I go to the old chest and rummage through it. A chess piece or a *santur* plectrum would be enough. But I return empty-handed.

Mother is as always sitting quietly on the bed, like a stick of dynamite whose long fuse is ignited. It's years that she's been like this. When you're constantly under such a gaze, you become anxious, you become cold, you freeze; the geranium leaves shake awkwardly, as if they are anxious too.

There isn't the slightest absentmindedness in mother; perhaps she's eradicated part of her life; then what's this tumultuous silence? No, she hasn't eradicated it, she's buried it in a corner of her mind: a corpse that doesn't rot away, doesn't become dust.

I get up and get out. The taxi driver says, 'From here on, it's a dirt road, if ...' The rest of his words swirl among the poplar trees on the two sides of the street; the sparrows fly away all of a sudden and all together.

I start walking, I reach my destination; grandfather takes a look at my dust-covered shoes.

'They don't regard this patch of road as a part of town; it's abandoned – no asphalt, no nothing.' And with his finger he shows me the brown piece of cloth beside the row of lined shoes.

We go into the room and sit; he offers me a piece of *nabaat*, I eat it although I don't feel like eating. I start out of the blue: 'Grandfather, a chess piece would do!'

He shakes his head. I say, 'A photograph, a letter or something.'

He is staring at me. Grandfather isn't a good liar; grandmother knew this very well, when she laughed and spoke about the days of their youth and of grandfather's innocent tricks, and how he would easily give himself away.

I say, 'Grandfather, this silence has got to be broken; the fuse of this dynamite is getting shorter every moment; it will finally explode; let me extinguish the fuse.'

He clutches at his white hair. He says, 'What do you know about her world, girl? How could she survive if she accepted it?'

'She will, she will! If she accepts it, then she'll bury her dead, cry for him, she'll calm down, she'll do whatever she wants to.'

Grandfather sighs and says, 'Yes, the earth is cold,' and keeps staring at grandmother's needlework on the wall. Suddenly he gets up, pushes aside the *qalamkar*[1] curtain hanging in the room, and seems to disappear; he's gone. In grandfather's absence, the room looks like a museum, a museum of memories: behind every object lie decades.

Grandfather's picture in the brown walnut frame shows him with an oiled and muscular body, as if he's Sohrab![2] His glance is

---

1. Fabric printed manually by means of wooden moulds and used as decorations in celebrations, tablecloths, furniture covers, carpet covers, bed sheets, curtains and garments. *Qalamkar* is traditionally made in the city of Isfahan, printed with figurative, abstract designs.

2. The protagonist of the *Tragedy of Rostam and Sohrab*, from the epic poetry book of Shahnameh, composed by great Iranian tenth century poet Ferdowsi. Sohrab is a symbol of youth, vigour and honesty.

the glance of Fathollah, the neighbourhood's mechanic: beautiful and shy – every time I look at him, he looks down and blushes, as if he knows that it's only in fairytales that he can fall in love with a student of painting!

Grandfather says, 'Here!'

When did he come in? When did the museum become a room again? I look at grandfather's worn-out figure and at his picture in the frame.

He hands me an old folded newspaper; I open it; there is another fold; I unfold it; the more I unfold it, the colour of the newspaper becomes paler. There is a picture inside it: like an image of the Chinese idol in a mysterious box!

A young man with smooth, soft, chestnut hair flowing on his forehead; there are two plectrums in a blurred movement between his fingers, and under his ample eyelids, there are eyes that I know are amber, and black long eyebrows.

'Your mother will have a heart attack if she sees this.'

'She won't, grandfather.'

'Yes, the earth is cold.'

And he looks at the picture in my hand and at the frame on the wall, which is full of small pictures set next to one another, like the patchwork that grandmother has sewn.

I hang the picture in a silver frame from the wall, facing mother. Mother suddenly shivers and with a strange voice that doesn't sound to be hers, she says, 'Where did you get it?'

'Out of my head, out of your head.'

She shouts, 'Take it away!' and her shout turns into a moan: 'Take it away, take it away.'

After years, she cries and moans quietly: 'My withered flower, hey, hey!' and she stares at my face with her red, sad eyes.

'Tea?' I ask.

I go into the kitchen; the sound of her quiet weeping is heard; again there's a sound of *santur*; it's the neighbouring boy who is practicing as usual, but this time I don't close the window and don't furtively look at mother! I take the tea. Mother is weeping quietly, 'Did he play like this? Hey, hey!'

She gets up and takes her pinky-white handkerchief from under her pillow; she approaches the wall, touches the frame with her mouth and pulls back: the glass has become misty; she runs the handkerchief over it gently.

Soft, chestnut hair appears, and there are eyes hidden under ample eyelids; I know they are amber.

ZOYA PIRZAD

The Stain

The woman put the knitting on her knee, bent her head back and slowly twisted her neck to the left and right. She could see the alley from where she was sitting. Children were playing football in the alley. The air was hot and suffocating. The woman rested her head against the back cushion and closed her eyes. She could distinguish each kid by his or her voice. This one was Ali, shouting, 'Pass the ball!' Mohammad was laughing his head off. Behrouz was yelling, 'Don't cheat, it was out!' and Khosrow shouted, 'That's the way, shoot!' There was a crying voice. It was Massoumeh, Mohammad's sister, who was incessantly wailing because the boys wouldn't let her join in the game. There was a sound of a bicycle bell. They had brought the evening paper. The woman moved her head on the cushion, pulled the familiar sounds of the alley and the hot summer air over her like a sheet, and lapsed into a nap.

Thirty years ago, with her husband she passed through the hubbub of the alley and entered this little house for the first time. That day too, kids were playing football in the alley. Perhaps they were fathers of Mohammad and Behrouz and Ali. A little girl was standing in a corner, crying. At that time, there was no jasmine pot in the courtyard. Neither were there little china statues on the mantle of the room. All these things appeared gradually later. First a pot of jasmine, then the second one – first a little statue of a gazelle, then another gazelle, then a tiny elephant with a trunk as thin as a needle. And with the passing of years, the woman little by little filled her little house with jasmine pots and statues and other things.

With the sounds of the days and the silence of the nights, the alley covered this familiar and fond collection like a foil. It had been thirty years that her life had carried on in the same way like a straight line, like the woollen knitting thread that was now lying in full length on the floor – thirty years with all of these years like the others, so also all the months and all the days, without a change, without an incident. The woman had no complaints in this regard. She was worried about incidents. With every simple bout of flu, she or her husband would be disturbed – not by a fear of disease, but by the change that would occur in their lives. She liked to know exactly what she was to expect every day and every hour. It took her ages to get accustomed to any change. Once when she bought a new saucepan, it remained in a corner of the kitchen until she finally convinced herself to cook in it, and the food she cooked in the new pan didn't taste nice to her palate.

The only incident in her life was her marriage. She hardly remembered the period before that. She had a blurred vision of her father and mother, both of whom had died years before she got married. Her life began from the first day of her marriage. But now she couldn't even remember that day properly. It seemed as if she had married on her birthday, or been born on her wedding day. She seldom thought about the days before her wedding. It was hard for her. As if thinking about something that didn't exist. As if thinking about some other person's life. When she stared at a handful of pictures from the past, she couldn't recognise herself.

The pale-faced girl in the pictures was a stranger to the middle-aged woman who looked at the pictures, lying in the heat of her fat body; the girl didn't stir any feeling in the woman's mind. Her life before marriage was as remote and blurred and unfamiliar to her as the period following it was vivid and easy to remember. It was as if all the years of that remote period were but one year, and all its months a single month, and all its days a single day – a day every single moment of which was familiar and sincere and close.

In the morning when she woke up, she turned on the radio before anything else. Then she laid the breakfast spread. The radio presenter read the news. The woman never listened to the news, but the presenter's voice was familiar and peaceful. When her husband left for work, she washed the dishes. Then she poured a cup of tea for herself, and with cup in hand, she walked through the house. She looked into the rooms, she went into the courtyard and sipped her tea and counted her day's tasks in her mind. Then she dressed up and went out shopping. She returned, tidied up the house, washed the clothes, ironed. Her husband didn't come home for lunch. The woman often ate the leftovers of the previous night's food. In the afternoons, she sometimes went to see neighbours and acquaintances: Soraya, whose mother had passed away; Mahin Khanom, who had just given birth.

They didn't have a child, and the woman had no complaints about it. Perhaps she was even glad. It was hard for her to imagine a new living being in the house. She would have to be sad for the kid, to be happy for it. She didn't like to be sad or happy. A child would disrupt the peace in the life, and the woman liked that peace more than anything else. In the late afternoon, after cooking dinner, she sat on the large cushion and listened to the sounds of the alley. A little before seven, she started looking into the alley, awaiting her husband's return. Their house was at the end of the alley, and from the window you could see the entire alley down to where it joined the street. At seven in the evening, the alley was usually dark and quiet and deserted. Only that part of the street that could be seen from the window was always alight, and far off from where the woman sat, the lights from neon signs and shop and cars intermingled, looking like a large luminous stain, around which the uproar of the street whirled fast and constantly like a halo. The woman didn't like the stain. When she kept staring at it for too long, the stain acquired bizarre and frightening forms and an ambiguous humming filled her ears. Sometimes she felt that the stain was getting closer and closer and larger and larger, until it seemed to be about to swallow her, and the unintelligible humming turned into a heinous laughter. Nevertheless, the woman had to look at the stain. Sooner or later, a dark dot would come out of it and approach her. The closer the dot came, the less the woman was scared. The dot gradually grew larger, transformed, and the woman saw her husband walking slowly towards home. This was the best moment of her day. A moment when a black and small dot completed the familiar and friendly collection of her life. She was no more scared of the big stain of light.

The woman opened her eyes. It had got dark. There was no sound in the alley. She looked at the clock. It was seven. The little black dot was halfway down the alley. The woman took in a deep breath and got up. She was to prepare the dinner.

Biographical Notes

Simin Daneshvar
Born 1931; novelist, short story writer, translator
Works include *Soovashoon, To Whom Shall I say Hello?* and *Island of Vagrancy*.

Goli Taraqqi
Born 1939; novelist, short story writer and poet
Works include *I AM Che Guevara, Hybernation, Somewhere Else* and *Fragmented Memories*.

Mahshid Amirshahy
Born 1931; novelist, short story writer, translator
Works include *Bibi Khanom's Starling, Mothers and Daughters*, and *After the Last Day*.

Mihan Bahrami
Born 1945; Writer, critic, painter and filmmaker
Works include *The Seven-horned Beast* and several volumes of children's stories.

Shahrnoosh Parsipour
Born 1946; Novelist and short story writer

Works include *The Dog and the Long Winter*, *Chrystal Pendants* and *Touba and the Meaning of the Night*.

Behjat Malek Kiani
Short story writer
Works published in literary periodicals

Fereshteh Molavi
Born 1954; writer, translator, librarian
Works include *A house of Clouds and Wind*, *Rey Sun* and *Persian Garden*.

Mansoureh Sharifzadeh
Born 1953; writer and translator
Works *include The Sixth Offspring* and *The Enamelled Mascara Case*.

Moniru Ravanipour
Born 1956; Writer
Works include *Kanizu*, *Heart of Steel*, and *Siria, Siria*.

Zohreh Hatami
Short story writer
Works include *New Stories*.

Farkhondeh Aqaei
Born 1956; Writer
Works include *One Woman, One Love*, and *The Lost Sex*.

Fereshteh Sari
Born 1956; Writer and poet
Works include *Echoes of Silence*, *Republic of Winter*, *Khatun* and *Mitra*.

Fariba Vafi
Born 1962; Writer and journalist
Works include *In the Depth of the Scene*, and *Even When We Laugh*.

Noushin Salari
Short story writer
Works published in literary periodicals.

Roya Shapourian
Born 1965; Writer
Works include *The Cheerful Face*, and *A Scrip of Stars*.

Qodsi Qazinoor
Short story writer
Works published in literary periodicals.

Zoya Pirzad
Born 1953; Writer
Works include *I Turn off the Lights* and *We Get Used to*.